WITHDRAWN

Binti: Home

BOOKS BY NNEDI OKORAFOR

THE BINTI TRILOGY
Binti
Binti: Home
Binti: The Night Masquerade

Remote Control
Who Fears Death
Kabu Kabu
Lagoon
The Book of Phoenix

YOUNGER READERS
Chicken in the Kitchen
Zahrah the Windseeker (as Nnedi Okorafor-Mbachu)
The Shadow Speaker (as Nnedi Okorafor-Mbachu)
Akata Witch
Akata Warrior
The Girl with the Magic Hands
Long Juju Man

NNEDI OKORAFOR

BINTI

HOME

A TOM DOHERTY ASSOCIATES BOOK

NEW YORK

This is a work of fiction. All of the characters, organizations, and events portrayed in this novella are either products of the author's imagination or are used fictitiously.

BINTI: HOME

Copyright © 2017 by Nnedi Okorafor

Edited by Lee Harris

A Tor.com Book
Published by Tom Doherty Associates
175 Fifth Avenue
New York, NY 10010

www.tor.com

Tor® is a registered trademark of
Macmillan Publishing Group, LLC.

ISBN 978-0-7653-9310-4 (ebook)
ISBN 978-1-250-20343-4 (hardcover)

First Edition: January 2017
First Hardcover Edition: July 2018

"Five five five five five five," I whispered. I was already treeing, numbers whipping around me like grains of sand in a sandstorm, and now I felt a deep click as something yielded in my mind. It hurt sweetly, like a knuckle cracking or a muscle stretching. I sunk deeper and there was warmth. I could smell the earthy aroma of the *otjize* I'd rubbed on my skin and the blood in my veins.

The room dropped away. The awed look on my mathematics professor Okpala's face dropped away. I was clutching my *edan*, the points of its stellated shape digging into the palms of my hands. "Oh, my," I whispered. Something was happening to it. I opened my cupped palms. If I had not been deep in mathematical meditation, I'd have dropped it, I'd not have *known* not to drop it.

My first thought was of a ball of ants I'd once seen tumbling down a sand dune when I was about six years old; this was how desert ants moved downhill. I had run to it for a closer look and squealed with disgusted glee at the undulating living mass of ant bodies. My *edan* was writhing and churning like that ball of desert ants now, the many triangular plates that it was made of flipping, twisting, shifting right there between my palms. The blue current I'd called up was hunting around and between them like a worm. This was a new technique that Professor Okpala had taught me and I'd gotten quite good at it over the last two months. She even called it the "wormhole" current because of the shape and the fact that you had to use a metric of wormholes to call it up.

Breathe, I told myself. The suppressed part of me wanted to lament that my *edan* was being shaken apart by the current I was running through it, that I should stop, that I would never be able to put it back together. Instead, I let my mouth hang open and I whispered the soothing number again, "Five five five five five." *Just breathe, Binti,* I thought. I felt a waft of air cross my face, as if something passed by. My eyelids grew heavy. I let them shut . . .

~

. . . *I was in space. Infinite blackness. Weightless. Flying, falling, ascending, traveling through a planet's ring of brittle metallic dust. It pelted my skin, fine chips of stone. I opened my mouth a bit to breathe, the dust hitting my lips. Could I breathe? Living breath bloomed in my chest from within me and I felt my lungs expand, filling with it. I relaxed.*

"Who are you?" a voice asked. It spoke in the dialect of my

family and it came from everywhere.

"Binti Ekeopara Zuzu Dambu Kaipka of Namib, that is my name," I said.

Pause.

I waited.

"There's more," the voice said.

"That's all," I said, irritated. "That's my name."

"No."

The flash of anger that spurted through me was a surprise. Then it was welcome. I knew my own name. I was about to scream this when . . .

~

. . . I was back in the classroom. Sitting before Professor Okpala. *I was so angry,* I thought. *Why was I so angry?* It was a horrible feeling, that fury. Back home, the priestesses of the Seven might even have called this level of anger unclean. Then one of my tentacle-like *okuoko* twitched. Outside, the second sun was setting. Its shine blended with the other sun's, flooding the classroom with a color I loved, a vibrant combination of pink and orange that the native people of Oomza Uni called "ntu ntu." Ntu ntu bugs were an Oomza insect who were a vibrant orange-pink that softly glowed in the dark.

The sunlight shined on my *edan,* which floated before

me in a network of current, a symmetry of parts. I'd never seen it disassemble like this and making it do so had not been my intention. I'd been trying to get the object itself to communicate with me by running current between its demarcations. Okpala claimed this often worked and I wanted to know what my *edan* would say. I had a moment of anxiety, frantically thinking, *Can I even put it back together?*

Then I watched with great relief as the parts of my *edan* that had detached slowly, systematically reattached. Whole again, the *edan* set itself down on the floor before me. *Thank the Seven,* I thought.

Both the blue from the current I still ran around it and the bright ntu ntu shined on Okpala's downturned face. She had an actual notebook and pencil in hand, so Earth basic. And she was writing frantically, using one of the rough thick pencils she'd made from the branch of the tamarind-like tree that grew outside the mathematics building.

"You fell out of the tree," she said, not looking up. This was how she referred to that moment when you were treeing and then suddenly were not. "What was that about? You finally had the *edan* willing to open itself."

"That's what it was doing? That was a good thing, then?"

She only chuckled to herself, still writing.

I frowned and shook my head. "I don't know . . . something happened." I bit my lip. "Something happened." When she looked up, she caught my eye and I had a moment where I wondered whether I was her student or a piece of research.

I allowed my current to fade, shut my eyes and rested my mind by thinking the soothing equation of $f(x) = f(-x)$. I touched the *edan*. Thankfully, solid again.

"Are you alright?" Professor Okpala asked.

Despite medicating with the soothing equation, my head had started pounding. Then a hot rage flooded into me like boiled water. "Ugh, I don't know," I said, rubbing my forehead, my frown deepening. "I don't think what happened was supposed to happen. Something happened, Professor Okpala. It was strange."

Now Professor Okpala laughed. I clenched my teeth, boiling. Again. Such fury. It was unlike me. And lately, it was *becoming* like me, it happened so often. Now it was happening when I treed? How was that even possible? I didn't like this at all. Still, I'd been working with Professor Okpala for over one Earth year and if there was one thing I should have learned by now it was that working with any type of *edan*, no matter the planet it had been found on, meant working with the unpredictable. "Everything comes with a sacrifice," Okpala liked to say. Every *edan* did something different for different reasons.

My *edan* was also poisonous to Meduse; it had been what saved my life when they'd attacked on the ship. It was why Okwu never came to watch any of my sessions with Okpala. However, touching it had no such effect on me. I'd even chanced touching my *okuoko* with my *edan*. It was the one thing that let me know that a part of me may now have been Meduse, but I was still human.

"That was isolated deconstruction," Professor Okpala said. "I've only heard of it happening. Never seen it. Well done."

She said this so calmly. *If she's never seen it happen before, why is she acting like I did something wrong,* I wondered. I flared my nostrils to calm myself down. No, this wasn't like me at all. My tentacle twitched again and a singular very solid thought settled in my mind: *Okwu is about to fight.* An electrifying shiver of rage flew through me and I jumped. Who was trying to bring him harm? Staining to sound calm, I said, "Professor, I have to go. May I?"

She paused, frowning at me. Professor Okpala was Tamazight, and from what my father said of selling to the Tamazight, they were a people of few but strong words. This may have been a generalization, but with my professor, it was accurate. I knew Professor Okpala well; there was a galaxy of activity behind that frown. However, I had to go and I had to go now. She held up a hand and waved it. "Go."

I got up and nearly crashed into the potted plant behind me as I turned awkwardly toward my backpack.

"Careful," she said. "You're weak."

I gathered my backpack and was off before she could change her mind. Professor Okpala was not head professor of the mathematics department for nothing. She'd calculated everything probably the day she met me. It was only much much later that I realized the weight of that brief warning.

~

I took the solar shuttle.

With the second sun setting, the shuttle was at its most charged and thus its most powerful. The university shuttle was snakelike in shape, yet spacious enough to comfortably accommodate fifty people the size of Okwu. Its outer shell was made from the molted cuticle of some giant creature that resided in one of the many Oomza forests. I'd heard that the body of the shuttle was so durable, a crash wouldn't even leave a scratch on it. It rested and traveled on a bed of "narrow escape," slick green oil secreted onto a track way by several large pitcher plants growing beside the station.

I'd always found those huge black plants terrifying,

they looked like they'd eat you if you got too close. And they surrounded themselves with a coppery stink that smelled so close to blood that the first time I came to the station, I had what I later understood was a panic attack. I'd stood on the platform staring blankly as I held that smell in my nose. Then came the flashes of memory from that time so vivid... I could smell the freshly spilled blood. Memories from when I was in the dining room of a ship in the middle of outer space where everyone had just been viciously murdered by Meduse.

I had not ridden the shuttle that day. I didn't ride it for many weeks, opting to take swift transport, a sort of hovering bus that was actually much slower and used for shorter journeys. When I couldn't stand the slowness and decided to try the solar shuttle again, I'd pinched my nose and breathed through my mouth until I got on-board. Once we started moving, the smell went away.

A native operated the scanner and I handed her my astrolabe to scan. She narrowed her wide blue eyes and looked at me down her small nose, as if she didn't see me take this shuttle often enough to know my schedule. She batted one of my *okuoko* with a finger; her hands were bigger than my head. Then she rubbed the *otjize* between her fingers and motioned for me to enter the shuttle's cabin.

I sat where I always sat, in the section for people my

size near one of the large round windows, and strapped myself in. The shuttle traveled five hundred to a thousand miles per hour, depending on how charged it was. I'd be in Weapons City in fifteen minutes and I hoped it wasn't too late, because Okwu was planning to kill his teacher.

~

The moment the house-sized lift rumbled open I ran out, my sandaled feet slapping the smooth off-white marble floor. The room was vast and high ceilinged with rounded walls, all cut into the thick toothlike marble. I coughed, my lungs burning. Wan, a Meduse-like person, was feet away, engulfed in a great lavender plume of its breathing gas. It didn't have Okwu's hanging tentacles, but Wan still looked like a giant version of the jellyfish who lived in the lake near my home on Earth. Wan also spoke Okwu's language of Meduse. I'd been down here plenty of times to meet Okwu, so it knew me, too.

"Wan, tell me where Okwu is," I demanded in Meduse.

It puffed its gas down the hallway. "There," Wan said. "Presenting to Professor Dema against Jalal today."

I gasped, understanding. "Thanks, Wan."

But Wan was already heading to the lift. I pulled my wrapper above my ankles and sprinted down the hallway. To my left and right, students from various parts of the galaxy were working on their own final projects of protective weaponry, the assignment this quarter. Okwu's was body armor, its close classmate Jalal's was electrical current.

Okwu and Jalal were taught together, stayed in the same dorm, and worked closely together on their projects. And today, they were being tested against each other, as was the way of Oomza Weapons Education. I was fascinated by the competitive push and pull of weapons learning, but I was glad mathematics was more about harmony. Okwu being Okwu—a Meduse of rigid cold honor, focus, and tradition—loved the program. The problem was that Okwu hated its professor and Professor Dema hated Okwu. Okwu was Meduse and Professor Dema, a human woman, was Khoush. Their people had hated and killed each other for centuries. Tribal hatred lived, even in Oomza Uni. And today that hatred, after simmering for a year, was coming to a head.

I reached the testing space just as Okwu, encased in a metallic skin, brought forth its white and sharp stinger and pointed it at Professor Dema. Feet away, Professor Dema stood, carrying a large gunlike weapon with both her hands and a snarl on her lips. This was not the way final exams were supposed to go.

"Okwu, what are you doing?" Jalal demanded in Meduse. She stood to the side, clutching a series of what looked like thick fire-tipped sticks with her mantislike claws. "You'll kill her!"

"Let us finish this once and for all," Okwu growled in Meduse. "Let me end you."

"Meduse have no respect," Okwu's professor said in Khoush. "Why they allowed you into this university is beyond me. You're unteachable."

"I've tolerated your insulting remarks all quarter. Let me end you. Your people should not plague this university," Okwu said.

My lungs were laboring from the gas Okwu was copiously pluming out as it prepared to attack its professor. If it didn't stop doing this, the entire room would be filled with it. I could see Professor Dema's eyes watering as she resisted coughing as well. I knew Okwu. It was doing this on purpose, enjoying the strained look on Professor Dema's face. I only had seconds to do something. I threw myself before Okwu, pressing myself to the floor before its *okuoko*, which hung just below its weaponized casing. I looked up at Okwu; its tentacles were soft and heavy on the side of my face. Meduse immediately understand prostration.

"Okwu, hear me," I said in Khoush. Since arriving at the university, I'd taught Okwu to speak Khoush and my language of Otjihimba and it hated the sound of both. My theory is that this was partially due to the fact that for

Okwu the sound of any language was inferior to Meduse. On top of this, Okwu had to produce the words through the tube between its *okuoko* that blew out the gas it used to breathe in air-filled atmospheres, and doing so was difficult and felt unnatural. Speaking to Okwu in Khoush was irritating to it and thus the best way to get its attention.

I called up a current, treeing faster than I ever could have back home. I'd learned much from Professor Okpala in the last year. My *okuoko* tickled, the current touching them and then reaching for Okwu's *okuoko*. Suddenly, I felt that anger again, and some part of me deep down firmly accused, "Unclean, Binti, you are unclean!" I gnashed my teeth as I fought to stay in control. When I could not, I simply let go. My voice burst from me clear and loud; in Khoush, I shouted, "Stop! Stop it right now!" I felt my *okuoko* standing on end, writhing like the clusters of mating snakes I often saw in the desert back home. I must have looked like a crazed witch; I felt like one, too.

Immediately, Okwu brought down its stinger, stopped pluming gas, and moved away from me. "Stay there, Binti," it said. "If you touch my casing, you will die."

Professor Dema brought down her weapon as well.

Silence.

I lay there on the floor, mathematics cartwheeling

through my brain, current still touching my only true friend on the planet even after a year. I felt the tension leave the room, leaving myself, too, finally. Tears of relief fell from the corners of my eyes as my strange random anger drained away. My *okuoko* stopped writhing. There were others in the cavernous workspace, watching. They would talk, word would spread, and this would be another reminder to students, human and nonhuman, to keep their distance from me, even if they liked me well enough.

Okwu's close classmate Jalal put down her weapons and hopped back. Professor Dema threw her gun to the floor and pointed at Okwu. "Your casing is spectacular. You will leave it here and download your recipe for it to my files. But if we meet outside this university where I am not your teacher and you are not my student, one of us will die and it will *not* be me."

I heard Okwu curse at her in Meduse so deep that I couldn't understand exactly what it said. Before I could admonish Okwu's crudeness, Professor Dema snatched up her weapon and shot at Okwu. It made a terrible boom that shook the walls and sent students fleeing. Except Okwu. The wall directly to its left now had a hole larger than Okwu's nine-foot-tall five-foot-wide jellyfish-like body. Chunks and chips of marble crumbled to the floor and dust filled the air.

"You didn't miss," Okwu said in Khoush. Its tentacles

shook and its dome vibrated. Laughter.

Minutes later, Okwu and I left the Weapons City In-verted Tower Five. Me with ringing ears and a headache and Okwu with a grade of Outstanding for its final pro-ject in Protective Gear 101.

~

Once on the surface, I looked at Okwu, wiped marble dust and *otjize* from my face, and said, "I need to go home. I'm going to go on my pilgrimage." I felt the air close to my skin; once I got back to my dorm room and washed up, I'd reapply my *otjize*. I'd take extra time to palm roll a thick layer onto my *okuoko*.

"Why?" Okwu asked.

I'm unclean because I left home, I thought. *If I go home and complete my pilgrimage, I will be cleansed. The Seven will forgive me and I'll be free of this toxic anger.* Of course, I didn't say any of this to Okwu. I only shook my head and stepped into the field of soft water-filled maroon plants that grew in the field over the Inverted Tower Five. Sometimes, I came here and sat on the plants, enjoying the feeling of buoyancy that reminded me of sitting on a raft in the lake back home.

"I'll come too," Okwu said.

I looked at it. "You'll land in a Khoush airport, if you're

even allowed on the ship. And they'll . . ."

"The treaty," it said. "I'll go as an ambassador for my people. No Meduse has been on Earth since the war with the Khoush. I'd be coming in peace." It thrummed deep in its dome and then added, "But if the Khoush make war, I will stir it with them, like you stir your *otjize*."

I grunted. "No need for that, Okwu. The peace treaty should be enough. Especially if Oomza Uni endorses the trip. And you come with me." I smiled. "You can meet my family! And I can show you where I grew up and the markets and . . . yes, this is a good idea."

Professor Okpala would certainly approve. A harmonizer harmonized. Bringing Okwu in peace to the land of the people its people had fought would be one of the ten good deeds Okpala had insisted I perform within the academic cycle as part of being a good Math Student. It would also count as the Great Deed I was to do in preparation for my pilgrimage.

Humans. Always Performing

Two weeks later, I powered up the transporter and said a silent prayer. The Seven were in the soil of my home and I was planets away from that home. Would they even hear me? I believed they would; the Seven could be in many places at once and bring all places with them. And they would protect me because I was a Himba returning home.

Still, my transporter did nothing. I stood there, out of breath, staring at the coin-sized flat stone. I'd rolled my hard-shelled pod into the lift and then across the dormitory hall to the entrance. The effort had left me sweaty and annoyed. Now this. The shuttle was a half-mile walk down the uneven rocky pathway. I'd been looking forward to the fresh air before the days on the ship. However, the walk wouldn't be so pleasant if I had to push my heavy traveling pod up the pathway. I knelt down and touched the transponder, again.

Nothing.

I pressed it hard, knowing this wouldn't yield any better result. It wasn't the pressure of the touch that activated it, but the contact with my index fingerprint.

Still nothing.

My face grew hot and I hissed with anger. I brought my foot back and kicked the transporter as hard as I could. It shot into the bushes. I froze with my mouth hanging open, astonished by my actions and the deep satisfaction they yielded. Then I ran to the bushes and started pushing the leaves near the ground this way and that, hoping to spot the tiny thing.

"Don't do that, you'll get all dirty before you're even on the ship," someone said from behind me as strong hands grasped my shoulders and gently pulled me back. It was Haifa, a Khoush student who was also studying weapons with Okwu. "Let me help you."

"All the way to the shuttle station?" I said, with a laugh.

"I've been studying all day," she said. "I need the exercise." She was wearing a tight green body suit made of a material so thin that I could see the bulging muscles on her long graceful arms and legs. Her astrolabe was attached to a clip sewn into her suit. As with the astrolabes of almost every student in my dorm, I'd tuned up its design and performance and now hers shined like polished metal and operated in a way more suited to her meticulous plodding way of thinking.

Haifa was much taller than me and one of those people who found motion so easy that she couldn't resist moving all the time. The day I met her, after asking me many questions about my *okuoko,* she'd told me that though she'd always been female, she'd been born physically male. Later, when she was thirteen, she'd had her body transitioned and reassigned to female. She'd joked that this process took longer than my getting stung in the back with a stinger to become part Meduse. "But it's why I get to be so tall," she'd bragged.

Every morning, she jogged several miles and then lifted logs at the lumberyard up the road. "The better to compete with people from other places," she now said, stepping to my pod. "Not easy being a human in the weapons department; we're so weak. Plus, I owe you," she said, gesturing to her astrolabe.

She started rolling my pod before I could say "yes," her thick black braids bouncing against her back. As she went, I swiped *otjize* from my forehead with my index finger, knelt down and touched the finger to the red Oomza soil, grounding the *otjize* into it. "Thank you," I whispered. I ran to catch up with Haifa, clutching my satchel to the side of my long silky red-orange wrapper.

"You think your family is going to like your new hairstyle?" Haifa asked, as she pushed and rolled the pod over the rocky path. A large succulent plant pulled in one of its branches as we passed it.

"It's not hair," I said. "They're—"

"I know, I know," she said, rolling her eyes. "Can't believe you allowed the Meduse to do that to you. Now you're Himba *and* one of those freaks. But I suppose it's better than dying."

I chuckled. "Much better."

"How come you're going home so soon, anyway?" she asked.

I stepped over a particularly large stone. "It's just time."

She looked over her shoulder at me as she rolled my pod. "Why isn't that monster here to help you? Does he know you're going?"

I rolled my eyes. "I'm meeting Okwu at the launch port."

"How did it score top of the class on the quarter final? I hear it paid off the professor."

I laughed, nearly jogging to keep up now. "Don't believe everything you hear."

"Or just carry a big gun at all times so that people will always tell the truth," she said, giving the pod a push.

About a hundred meters from the shuttle station, Haifa decided to outdo herself by picking up my pod and sprinting with it. When she reached the front of the shuttle station, she put the pod down, did a graceful backflip, and gleefully jumped up and clicked her heels. A few people waiting at the shuttle platform applauded with whistles, flashes of light, and slapping tentacles. Haifa took a dramatic bow for them. "I am amazing," she declared, as I walked up to her.

A person who looked like a two-foot-tall version of a praying mantis clicked its powerful forelegs. In a sonorous voice, it said, "Humans. Always performing."

The shuttle arrived, gliding on the smooth green oil path, and the five people waiting crowded quickly onboard. I was last to board, pinching my nose to avoid the blood smell of the pitcher plants. Haifa loaded my pod inside for me, gave me a tight hug, and leapt through the large round shuttle window near the entrance like a missile. Moments later, the shuttle got moving; it never waited for long. "Tell Okwu I send my insults!" Haifa shouted as the shuttle passed her. She started to run alongside the shuttle and for a moment, she kept up.

"I will," I said.

"Safe travels, Binti! No fear, Master Harmonizer, you belong in space!" Haifa shouted and then the shuttle left her in its wake of blasted air, which blew her thick braids back. Holding on to the rail beside me, I turned and watched as we sped away from her. She did one more flip and waved enthusiastically. Then she was gone because we'd reached the day's cruising speed of seven hundred miles per hour.

I stood there for a moment, feeling the usual moment of lightheadedness as the shuttle stabilized its passengers, and then I quickly went to my assigned window seat. I had to squeeze past two furry individuals and they protested when my *otjize* rubbed off on their furry feet and one of my *okuoko* brushed one in the furry face.

"Sorry," I said, in response to their growls.

"We've heard about you," one said in gruff Meduse. "You're a hero, but we didn't know you were so . . . soily."

"It's not soil, its—" I sighed and smiled and just said, "Thank you." Both of their astrolabes began to sing. They grabbed them and began another conversation among themselves and four others projected before them in a language I didn't understand. I sat down and turned to the window.

Fifteen minutes later, when we stopped in Weapons City, I met up with Okwu, who was coming from a meeting with its professor; somehow the two hadn't killed each other and I was thankful. *One day the Meduse and the Khoush will get over themselves,* I thought. The new treaty was a good start.

An hour later, we arrived at the launch station. And that's when I began to feel ill.

~

The three university medical center doctors who'd examined me said I was suffering from post-traumatic stress disorder because of what happened on the ship last year. For the first few weeks, I was okay, but eventually I started having nightmares, day terrors, I'd see red and then Heru's chest bursting open. Sometimes, just looking at Okwu made me want to vomit, though I never told it this was happening. And then there were the random instances of intense focused fury that invaded my usually calm mind.

Eventually, Okwu and I were ordered by the departments of mathematics and weapons to see therapists. Okwu never mentioned how its sessions went and I didn't ask. You just don't ask a Meduse about such things. I doubt it told any of its family, either. In turn, Okwu never asked about my sessions.

My therapist was named Saidia Nwanyi. She was a short squat Khoush woman who liked to sing to herself when no one was around. I learned this on my first visit to her office. It was in Math City, so a five-minute walk from my class. I was uncomfortable that day. Similar to the Meduse, in my family, one does not go to a stranger and spill her deepest thoughts and fears. You go to a family member and if not, you hold it in, deep, close to the heart, even if it tore you up inside. However, I wasn't home and the university was not making seeing a therapist a choice, it was an order. Plus, despite the fact that it made me extremely uncomfortable, I knew I needed help.

So I went and as I approached her office, I heard her singing. I stopped and listened. Then the tears came. The song she sang was an old Khoush song the women, Khoush or Himba, sang as they went into the desert to hold conversation with the Seven. I'd heard my mother sing it for weeks whenever she returned. I'd heard my oldest sister sing it to herself, as she polished astrolabe parts for the shop. I'd sung the song to myself whenever I snuck into the desert.

I entered Dr. Nwanyi's office with wet cheeks and she'd smiled, firmly shaken my hand, and closed the door behind me. That first day, we talked for an hour about my family, Himba customs, and the rigid expectations placed especially on girls in both Himba and Khoush families. She was so easy to talk to and I learned more about the Khoush that day than I had in my entire life. In some ways, Himba and Khoush were like night and day, but in matters of girlhood and womanhood and control, we were the same. What a surprise this was to me. That first day, we didn't talk about what happened on the ship at all and I was glad. Afterward, I walked to my dorm room feeling like I'd visited a place close to home.

Eventually, we did go deep into my experiences on the ship and doing so brought up such rawness. Over those months with Dr. Nwanyi, I learned why sleep was so difficult, why my heart would beat so hard for no reason, why I had such a tough time at solar shuttle platforms, and why I couldn't bear the thought of boarding a ship. But now, something had shifted in me. I was ready to go home. I needed to go home.

The day after the showdown between Okwu and its professor, I'd made an appointment with Haras, the University Chief. When we met, I told it how urgent my need was and Haras understood. Within a week, the university had given Okwu permission to travel and gained agreement from the Khoush city of Kokure and my hometown of Osemba to allow Okwu to visit as an ambassador. Okwu would be the first Meduse to come to Khoushland in peace.

The swiftness of these arrangements astonished me, but I moved with it all. One does not question good fortune. Home was calling, as was the desert into which I would go with the other Himba girls and women on pilgrimage. Okwu and I were issued tickets to Earth not long after quarter's end. My therapist, Dr. Nwanyi, hadn't wanted me to go so soon, but I insisted and insisted and insisted.

"Just make sure you breathe," she'd said as I left her office hours before the journey. "Breathe."

Launch

I followed Okwu through the enormous entrance to the Oomza Uni West Launch Port. Immediately, my sharp eyes found the doorways to docked ships far beyond the drop-off zone, ticketing and check-in stations and terminals. I opened my mouth to take in a deep lungful of air and instead coughed hard; Okwu had just decided to let out a large puff of its gas.

When I finally stopped coughing and my eyes focused on the docked ships, my heart began to beat like a talking drum played by the strongest drummer. I rubbed some *otjize* with my index finger from my cheek and brought it to my nose and inhaled, exhaled, inhaled, exhaled its sweet aroma. My heart continued its hard beat, but at least it slowed some. Okwu was already at check-in and I quickly got behind him.

The Oomza West Launch Port was nothing like the Kokure Launch Port back home. The hugeness of it was breathtaking. Since coming to Oomza Uni, I'd seen buildings of a size that I couldn't previously have imagined. The vastness of the desert easily surpassed these structures, but where the desert was a creation of the Seven, these buildings were not.

The great size of the Oomza West Launch Port was secondary to the great diversity of its travelers. Back at Kokure, almost every traveler and employee was human and I had been the only Himba in a sea of Khoush. Here, everyone was everything . . . at least to my still fresh eyes. I was seventeen years old and I had been at Oomza Uni for only one of those years now, having spent the previous all on Earth among my self-isolating Himba tribe in the town of Osemba. I barely even knew the Khoush city of Kokure, though it was only thirty miles from my home.

The launch port was like a cluster of bubbles, each section its own waiting space for those in transit. There were whole terminals that I could not enter, because the gas they were filled with was not breathable to me. One terminal was encased in thick glass and the inside looked as if it were filled with a wild red hurricane, the people inside it flying about like insects.

Just from standing in line and looking around, I saw people of many shapes, sizes, organisms, wavelengths, and tribes here. I saw no humans like me, though. And if I *had* seen a fellow Himba, it was doubtful that I'd see any with Meduse tentacles instead of hair. Being in this place of diversity and movement was overwhelming, but I felt at home, too . . . as long as I didn't look at the ships.

"Binti and Okwu?" the ticketing agent enthusiastically said in Meduse through a small box on her large dome. She was a creature somewhat like Okwu, jellyfish-like and the size of a storage shed, except her dome was a deep shade of black and she had antennae at the center with a large yellow eye. Over the last year, I'd learned (well, brashly been told) that the females of this group of people had the long antenna with the yellow eyes. The males simply had a large green eye on their domes, no antenna. This one used her eye to stare at Okwu and me with excitement.

"Yes," I responded in the language of my people.

"Oh, how exciting," she said, switching to Otjihimba too. "I will tell all my male mates about today . . . and maybe even a few of my female ones, too!" She paused for a moment looking at her astrolabe sitting on the counter and then the screen embedded in the counter. The screen hummed softly and complex patterns of light flashed on it and moved in tiny rotating circles. As I watched, my harmonizer mind automatically assigned numbers to each shape and equations to their motions. The agent switched back to Meduse, "Today, you'll be—" She paused, pluming out a large burst of gas. I frowned. "You will both be traveling on the human-geared ship, the Third Fish. Do you . . ."

The talking drum in my chest began to beat its rhythm of distress, again.

"That's the ship we came in on," Okwu said.

"Yes. She may have experienced tragedy that day, but she still loves to travel."

I nodded. The Third Fish was a living thing. Why should she die or stop flying because of what happened? Still, of all ships for us to travel on, why the same one inside which so much death had happened and we'd both nearly died?

"Is . . . is this alright?" the agent asked. "The university has given you two lifetime travel privileges, we can put you on any ship . . . but the time may . . ."

"I do not mind," Okwu said.

I nodded. "Okay. Me neither. The spirits and ghosts of the dead don't stay where they're freed." I felt my right eye twitch slightly.

"Great," the ticketing agent said. "You've both been given premium rooms near the pilot quarters."

I hesitated and then stepped forward. "Is there any way I can have . . . the room I had on the way here?"

The agent's eye bent toward me and she plumed out a small cloud of gas. "Why? I . . . I mean, are you sure?"

I nodded.

"It's quite small and near the servant quarters," the agent said. "And the security doors are . . ."

"I know," I said. "I want that room."

The agent nodded, looked at her astrolabe and then the screen. "I can get you the room, but I hope you are okay with it being in a slightly different place."

I frowned. "I don't understand."

"The Third Fish is pregnant and will probably give birth when she arrives on Earth. The newborn will be a great asset to the Earth Miri 12 Fleet, of course. What's good for passengers is that her pregnancy means the Third Fish will travel faster. But it also means her inner rooms and chambers shift some and will be a little more cramped."

"Why will she travel faster?" I asked out of pure curiosity.

"The sooner she'll get to Earth to bear her child," the agent said with a grin. "Isn't it fascinating?"

I nodded, also smiling. It really was.

~

"We're honored to have you both aboard," the boarding security guard said to me in Khoush a half-hour later, after our long walk to the gate. He was human and looked about the age of my father. He had a long beard and white Khoush-style robes. My fast-beating heart flipped just seeing him. Few on Oomza Uni dressed like this and, suddenly, home felt closer than ever.

"Thank you, sir," I said, handing him my astrolabe to scan. On Oomza Uni, all humans and many nonhumans used astrolabes and they were scanned so regularly that doing so no longer bothered me as it had that very first time when I'd left home.

I glanced back at Okwu and whispered, "Say thank you or something." But Okwu said nothing. It clearly didn't appreciate the guard not bothering to look at or speak directly to it in its language.

"Meduse are too proud to use astrolabes, so this part of security does not apply to it," the guard said, clearly picking up on Okwu's irritation. He handed back my astrolabe.

As I took it, I looked past him at the entrance to the Third Fish. The hallway leading inside was the same warm blue it had been that fateful day over a year ago. "Sure," I said, with a wave of my hand. "It's fine." *Was it blue when I exited?* I wondered, as I put my astrolabe into my pocket next to my *edan*. I couldn't remember; I hadn't been paying attention. I'd had other things to worry about, like trying to prevent a battle. Something red caught my eye on the security guard's uniform. A breath caught in my chest as I focused on the small red beetle. It walked right over where the man's heart would be. Red point on white. Red point. On white. I frowned, knowing what was coming, but unable to stop it. The flashback that hit me was so strong I twitched.

Heru's narrow chest.

His kaftan was white.

A red dot appeared on it like a cursor on a blank screen.

On the left side.

Left side.

Left side. Where his heart lived.

It had been beating. Calm. Happy.

Then it was a muscle, torn through.

The Meduse stinger was white and blood stained it easily.

That red dot bloomed like a rose on the bushes that liked to grow in the desert.

Heru's blood. Some spattered on my face. As his heart tore, as my mind broke.

Five five five five five five five five five five five five five five five five five five five.

"Binti of Namib?" the guard asked.

I'd spoken with Heru's parents twice. The first time, his mother only gazed at me through the virtual screen and cried. Openly, unflinchingly, she'd stared at me as if she could reach out and touch her son through my eyes. The second time, Heru's brother, only a year younger than Heru, called and demanded I recount every detail of the last moment. He didn't care that it made me weep or that it would lead to a full week of nightmare-packed nights for me. And neither did I. Heru's brother looked so much like him, same granite black hair and bushy eyebrows. After those two calls, I heard nothing from Heru's people.

"Binti of Namib?" the guard asked, again.

"Oh," I said, looking up. I shook myself a bit. "Sorry."

"You may board the ship."

"Thank you," I said. I turned to Okwu and I had to stare at it for several seconds, as I prevented myself from falling into another nasty flashback, this one involving Okwu and how it had initially tried to kill me. Then I said to it in Meduse, "You first, my friend."

~

Crossing the threshold and stepping onto the ship was easy enough. I felt the talking drum in my chest, but that was all. Okwu floated off to its room on the other side of the ship and I was glad to be alone. I needed to be alone. I needed to experience *this* alone.

I passed a few people in the hallway to the sleeping rooms. It felt strange to be among so many humans again. Too quiet. I clutched my silky shawl closer to my body, feeling people's eyes on my *okuoko* and my *otjize*-covered skin, especially my arms, neck, and face. Even among the many races at Oomza Uni, it had been a long time since I'd felt so alien.

I started my breathing techniques the moment I saw my room's door; if I began treeing, I'd never experience the full effect of my terror and thus wouldn't be able to address it properly. This was one of Dr. Nwanyi's requests, not in this moment (she hadn't wanted me to take this trip), but in the idea. "When you face your deepest fears, when you are ready," she'd said. "Don't turn away. Stand tall, endure, face them. If you get through it, they will never harm you again."

I took deep, lung-filling breaths as I approached the door. Still, a violent shudder ran through my body and I leaned against the golden wall for support. "Everything is fine," I whispered in Otjihimba. I switched to Meduse, "Everything is fine." But everything wasn't fine. I was walking toward the door, my back stiff, my mind full of equations. I was carrying a tray heavy with food from the dining hall, and everyone on the ship was dead. Chests torn open by Meduse stingers; the Meduse had enacted *moojh-ha ki-bira,* the "great wave."

Leaning against the wall, I pushed myself within feet of my room's door. A woman with a staring small child walked by, greeted me, and entered her room doors away. The hallway grew quiet as the woman's door locked behind her. The *shhhhhp* of the door sealing itself seemed to echo all around me. I began to see stars through my watering eyes.

Heru.

He was lovely. I liked him.

Then his eyes changed because a Meduse ripped through his heart. All my friends who should have been in my class. Dead. I am the only human on Oomza of my year because all others are dead. All dead. All dead.

I smelled their blood now. Heard the ripping. No screams, because that required un-torn lungs. Gasps. Spilling. I'd come here. My choice.

I held my *otjize*-covered hands to my nose and tried to inhale the sweet scent, flowers, clay, tree oils. But I couldn't breathe. I pressed my hands to my chest, as if I could cup my own beating un-torn heart, as if I could calm it. For a moment, everything went black. Then my sight cleared. I whimpered.

"Shallow breaths, increased heart rate, you're having a panic attack," a stiff female voice said in Khoush.

"I am," I whispered. I didn't like for my astrolabe to speak, but Professor Okpala had had me set it to speak whenever I had a panic attack. I'd protested back then, but now I understood why.

"I suggest you drop into mathematical meditation." The voice was coming from my pocket, in which my astrolabe was warming and vibrating gently.

"If I . . . do, I learn . . . nothing," I gasped.

"There is time to learn, Binti," the voice said. "This

won't be your last panic attack. But there's no one in this hallway but me and all I can do is notify the ship's medics. Help yourself, drop into meditation right now."

Everything went black, again. And when things came back, no matter how hard I tried, I couldn't stop seeing Meduse stingers tearing through bodies with surprised faces. Heru, Remi, Olu ... I could not force myself to inhale and get air into my lungs. My chest was burning when I finally gave in. I "slipped into the trees" and dropped into meditation.

Ahhhhh ...

The numbers flew, split, doubled, spun like the voice of the Seven.

And soon they were everywhere and everything.

I grabbed at Euler's identity, $e^{i \times \pi} + 1 = 0$, and I went from plummeting to gently floating down a warm rabbit hole with soft furry walls and landing on a bed of pillows and flowers. When I looked up from this fragrant quiet place, the narrowed telescopic view made things above clearer. I was on the Third Fish, a peaceful giant who was like a shrimp and could breathe in outer space because of internal rooms full of oxygen-producing plants that served as lungs. The violent death of many had happened on this ship, of my teacher, my friends, but not for me. No, not for me. I'd lived. And I'd become family with the murderous Meduse.

"Mmmmm," I said, from deep within my chest. My heart beat slowly. I reached into my pocket and brought out my *edan*. Quietly, I whispered my favorite equation and the blue current etched into the *edan*'s fractals of fine grooves and lines. I still did not know what it was, but after studying with Professor Okpala and studying the *edan* itself, I knew how to make it speak and later sing. I went to my room's door and let the door scan my eyes. It opened and I stepped into the room where I had learned to survive.

~

My first sleeping cycle (for there isn't any night and day in space, let alone ones that are on Earth time) was full of violent nightmares so sharp that I could barely tolerate being around Okwu the next day. I'd never told it about my panic attacks or nightmares and I didn't tell it now.

Such things did not move Okwu and all it would say was that these would not kill me and I should strengthen myself and push past it all. Meduse don't understand the human condition; my emotional pain would only irritate Okwu when it couldn't make my pain instantly better. So, instead, I kept my distance from it that first day, saying I needed time to think. The ship had a separate gas-filled dining hall for Okwu and it found the food there so delicious that it spent most of that first day there. Being on the ship had no effect on Okwu; it felt right at home and easily reveled in the luxuries the ship and the university provided.

I didn't analyze this too closely. If I went down that desert hare's burrow, I'd find myself in a dark dark place where I asked questions like, "Who did Okwu kill during the *moojh-ha ki-bira*?" I understood that when Okwu had participated in the killing, it had been bound by the strong Meduse thread of duty, culture, and tradition . . . until my *otjize* showed it something outside of itself.

During those first months at Oomza Uni, Okwu had answered my calls and walked for miles and miles with me through Math City during the deepest part of night when I suffered from homesickness so powerful that all I could do was walk and let my body think I was walking home. It had talked me into contacting all my siblings, even when I was too angry and neglected to initiate contact. Okwu had even allowed my parents to curse and shout at it through my astrolabe until they'd let go of all their anger and fear and calmed down enough to finally ask it, "How is our daughter?" Okwu had been my enemy and now was my friend, part of my family. Still, I requested that my meals be delivered to my room.

By the second day, the flashbacks retreated and I was able to spend time with Okwu talking in the space between our dining halls.

"It's good to be off planet again," Okwu said.

I gazed out the large window into the blackness. "This is only my second time," I said.

"I know," Okwu said. "That's why being on Oomza Uni was so natural for you. I enjoy the university with its professors and students, but for me, it's left me feeling . . . heavy."

I turned to it, smiling. "But you're so . . . light already. You barely weigh . . ."

"It's not about mass and gravity," it said, twitching its *okuoko* in amusement. "It's the way you feel about needing to be near the desert. You don't live in it, but you played in it a lot and you like living near its vastness. It is always there. It is the same with me and space."

I nodded, thinking of the desert near my home. "I understand. Is that why you wanted to come with me so badly?"

It puffed out a plume of gas. "I can travel home at any time," it said. "But the timing seemed right. The chief likes the idea of irritating the Khoush with my visit." It shook its tentacles and vibrated its domes, laughter.

"You're coming to make trouble?" I asked, frowning.

"Meduse like war, especially when one isn't allowed to make war." A ripple of glee ran up the front of its dome.

I grunted turning away from it and said in Otjihimba,

"There isn't going to be any war."

Three Earth days. When it came time to eat, though I tried, things didn't get any better. I took one step into the dining hall where the Meduse had performed *moojh-ha ki-bira*, looked around, turned and went right back to my room, and again requested my meals to be sent there.

I spent much of my time meditating in the ship's largest breathing chamber. Most were not allowed to enter these spaces for more than a highly monitored few minutes, but my unique hero status got me whatever I wanted, including unlimited breathing room time. Okwu didn't join me here because its gas wasn't good for the plants, plus it didn't like the smell of the air. For me, the fragrant aroma of the many species of oxygen-producing plants and the moist air required to keep them alive was perfect for my peace of mind. And the *otjize* on my skin remained at its most velvety smooth here.

The remaining days passed, as time always does when you are alive, whether happy or tortured. And soon, I was strapping myself in my black landing chair and watching the earth get closer and closer.

When we entered the atmosphere, the sunlight touched my skin and the sweet familiar sensation brought tears to my eyes. Then my *okuoko* relaxed on my shoulders as I felt the sunshine on them for the first time.

Even being what they were, my *okuoko* knew the feeling of home. After we landed and the ship settled at its gate, I sat back and looked out the window at the blue sky.

I laughed.

At Home

Before we'd left, Oomza University Relations instructed Okwu and me to wait two hours for everyone to exit the ship before we did when we arrived on Earth.

"But why?" I'd asked.

"So there is no trouble," both of the reps we'd been meeting with had said simultaneously.

It had been over a hundred years since a Meduse had come to Khoush lands, and never had one arrived in peace. The reps told us the launch port would be cleared for exactly one hour, except for my family, representatives, officials, and media from the local Khoush city of Kokure and my hometown of Osemba. A special shuttle would drive Okwu, me, and my family to my village.

The two hours we waited allowed me to shake off my landing weakness. I wore my finest red long stiff wrapper and silky orange top, my *edan* and astrolabe nestled deep in the front pocket of my top. I'd also put all my metal anklets back on. I did a bit of my favorite traditional dance before my room's mirror to make sure I'd put them on well. The fresh *otjize* I'd rubbed on every part of my body felt like assuring hands. I'd even rolled three of Okwu's *okuoko* with *otjize*; this would please my family, even if it annoyed the Khoush people. To Meduse, touching those hanging long tentacles was like touching a human's long hair, it wasn't all that intimate, but Okwu wouldn't let just anyone touch them. But it let me. Covering them with so much *otjize,* Okwu told me, made it feel a little intoxicated.

"Everything is . . . happy," it had said, sounding per-plexed about this state.

"Good," I said, grinning. "That way, you won't be so grumpy when you meet everyone. Khoush like polite-ness and the Himba expect a sunny disposition."

"I will wash this off soon," it said. "It's not good to feel this pleased with life."

We walked down the hallway and when we rounded a curve, it opened into the ship's exit. For a moment, I could see everyone out there before they saw me. Three news drones hovered feet away from the entrance. The carpeting before the exit was a sharp red. I blinked and touched my forehead, pushing, shoving the dark thoughts away.

I spotted my family, standing there in a group, then an-other group of Khoush and Himba welcoming officials. I hadn't told my family about my hair not being hair anymore, that it was now a series of alien tentacles resulting from the Meduse genetics being introduced to mine; that they had sensation and did other things I was still coming to understand. I could hide my *okuoko* with *otjize,* especially when I spoke with my family through my astrolabe where they couldn't see how my *okuoko* sometimes moved on their own. *Won't be able to hide them for long now,* I thought.

Any moment, I would exit and they would all see me. I slowed down and took a deep breath, let it out and took in another. I held a hand out behind me for Okwu to wait. Then I knelt down, swiped some *otjize* from my cheek, and touched it to the ship's floor. My prayer to the Seven was brief and wordless but within it, I asked them to bless the Third Fish, too. "This interstellar traveling beast holds a part of my soul," I whispered. "Please give her a safe delivery and may her child be heavy, strong, as adventurous as her mother and as lovely." I wished the Third Fish could understand me and thus understand my thanks and I felt one of my *okuoko* twitch. As if in response, the entire ship rumbled. I gasped, grinning, delighted. I pressed my palm more firmly to the floor. Then I stood and walked to the exit.

I stepped out of the ship before Okwu, so the sound of my mother's scream reached my ears immediately.

"Binti!" Then there was a mad rush and I was suddenly in a crush of bodies, half of them covered in *otjize* (only the women and girls of the Himba use the *otjize*). Mother. Father. Brothers. Sisters. Aunts. Uncles. Cousins.

"My daughter is well!"

"Binti!"

"We've missed you!"

"Look at you!"

"The Seven is here!"

When everyone let go, I started sobbing as I clung to my mother, holding my father's hand as he followed close behind. I caught my brother Bena's eye as he flicked one of my *otjize*-heavy locks with his hand. Thankfully, this didn't hurt much. "Your hair has grown," he said. I grinned at him, but said nothing. My sisters started swinging their long thick *otjize*–palm rolled locks side to side and singing a welcome song, my brothers clapping a beat.

And then it all stopped. I stopped in mid-sob. My parents stopped joyously laughing. Bena was looking behind me with wide eyes, his mouth agape as he pointed. I slowly turned around. For a moment, I was two people—a Himba girl who knew her history very very well and a Himba girl who'd left Earth and become part-Meduse in space. The dissonance left me breathless.

Okwu filled the exit with its girth. Its three *otjize*-covered *okuoko* were waving about, as if in zero gravity, one of them whipping before its dome violently, as if signing some sort of insult. Its light blue semitransparent thin-fleshed dome was protected by the clear metal armor it'd created on Oomza Uni. From the bottom front of its dome protruded its large white toothlike stinger.

Behind me, I heard clattering and the sound of booted footsteps rushing into the room. When I turned, one of the Khoush soldiers had already brought forth his gun and fired it. *Bam!* Screams, running, someone or maybe some two were grabbing and pulling at me. I dug in my heels, yanked at my arms. A small burst of fire bloomed in the carpet at Okwu's tentacles. Inches from Okwu, feet from the Third Fish.

"What are you doing?" I shouted. *Oh no,* I thought, a moan in my gut. I felt Okwu's rage flare, a burning in my scalp, a fire igniting in me, as well. The anger. *Not in front of my family! Unclean, unclean,* I thought. *I was unclean.* Okwu made no sound or move, but I knew in moments, every soldier, maybe every *one* in this room would be dead ... except possibly me. The Meduse do not kill family, but did that include "family through battle?"

I pulled from my mother's grasp, hearing the sleeve

of my top rip. I pushed my father aside, grabbed my wrapper, and lifted it above my knees. Then I ran. Past my family, dodging news drones, who turned to watch me. I flung myself in the space between Okwu and the line of soldiers that had flooded in from a doorway on the left. I let go of my wrapper and thrust my hands out, one palm facing the soldiers and the other facing Okwu.

"Stop!" I screamed. I shut my eyes. Okwu was going to strike; would it notice that it was I? Was I Meduse enough to avoid its stinger? Oh, my family. The Khoush soldiers were already shooting, the fire bullets would tear and burn me from inside out. Still, I stood up straight, my mind clear and crisp; I'd forgotten to drop into meditation.

Silence.

Eyes closed, I heard not even a footstep or rustle of someone's garments or Okwu's whipping tentacles. Then I did hear something and felt it, too. *Oh, not here,* I thought, my heart sinking as it drummed too fast and too hard. It had happened once before on Oomza Uni. I was in the forest digging up clay to make my *otjize* when a large piglike beast came running at me. It was too late to make a dash for it, so I froze and looked it in the eyes. The beast stopped, sniffed me with its wet snout, rubbed its rough brown furry rump against my arm, lost interest, and walked off.

As I watched it disappear into a bush, I noticed my long *okuoko* were writhing on my head like snakes, very much like Okwu's were now as it stood in the exit, stinger ready. I could hear my *okuoko* now, softly vibrating and warming. If I created a current while in this state, there would be sparks popping from the tips of each *otjize*-covered tentacle.

"Oh my Gods, is she part Meduse now?" I heard someone ask.

"Maybe she's its wife," I heard one of the journalists whisper back.

"The Himba are a filthy people," the person said. "That's why they shouldn't be allowed to leave Earth." Then there was snickering.

I met my father's eyes and all I saw was intense raw terror. His eyes quickly moved to Okwu and I knew he was looking at its stinger. I saw the faces of my family and all the other Himba and Khoush here to welcome me and I saw the history lessons kick in as they lay their eyes on the first Meduse they had ever seen in real life.

"Okwu is—" I turned from the soldiers to Okwu and back, trying to speak to them all at the same time. "All of you . . . don't move! If you move . . . Okwu . . . calm down, Okwu! You fight now, you kill everyone in here.

These are my family, my people, as you are . . . We'll remain alive and there will be a chance for all of us to grow as . . . as people." Sweat beaded through the *otjize* on my face and tumbled down my cheeks. More silence. Then a soft slippery sound; Okwu sheathing its stinger. Thank the Seven.

"I have respected your wishes, Binti," Okwu said coolly in Meduse.

I turned to the Khoush and spoke quickly. "This is Okwu, Meduse ambassador and student of Oomza Uni. The Pact. Remember the *Pact*. Have you forgotten? It's law. Please. He is here in *peace* . . . unless treated otherwise. Please. We're a people of honor, too." As I stared forcefully at the Khoush soldiers, I couldn't help but feel hyperaware of the *otjize* on my face and the fact that they probably all saw me as a near savage.

Still, after a moment, the soldier in front raised a hand and motioned for the others to stand down. I let out a great sigh of relief and lowered my chin to my chest. "Praise the Seven," I whispered. My mother began to clap furiously, and soon everyone else did, too. Including some of the soldiers.

"Welcome to Earth," a tall Khoush man in immaculate white robes said, sweeping in, grabbing my hand and pumping it. He spoke with the gusto of a politician who's just had the wits scared from him. "I am Truck Omaze, Kokure's new mayor. It's a great honor to have you arriving at our launch port on your way home. You're an inspiration to all of us here on Earth, but especially in this part of the world."

"Thank you, Alhaji," I said, politely, straining to control my quivering voice.

"These Meduse," I heard my father tell my mother. "Look how the Khoush are afraid of just one. If I didn't feel I was going to die of terror, I'd be laughing."

"Shush!" my mother said, elbowing him.

"Come, let us smile to everyone." His grin was false and his grasp was tight as he laughingly whirled me toward the news drones, without giving Okwu a single glance. The mayor smelled of perfumed oil and I was reluctant to get too close to him with his white robes. However, he didn't seem to mind the *otjize* stains, or maybe he was so shaken that he didn't care at the moment. He pulled me close as the drones moved in and his grin broadened. I felt him shudder as Okwu moved in behind us to get into the shots. And despite the fact that we'd all nearly been on the verge of death by fire bullet or stinger or both, I somehow grinned convincingly at the camera drones.

~

We had about forty-five minutes and both Himba and Khoush journalists sat us down right there in a vacated airport restaurant for interviews. From the questions, I gathered what the community most wanted to know.

"We are proud of you, will you stay?"

"You have befriended the enemy. Will you meet with our elders and share your wisdom?"

"What was your favorite food on Oomza Uni?"

"What are you studying?"

"What kind of fashion are you most interested in now?"

"Why did you come back?"

"They let you come back? Why?"

"Why did you abandon your family?"

"What are those things on your head? Are you still Himba?"

"You still bless with *otjize,* why?"

"Mathematics, astrolabes, and a mysterious object, you're truly amazing. Will you be staying now that you've seen Oomza Uni, a place so much greater than your meager Himba home?"

"What was Oomza Uni like for a tribal girl like you?"

"What is that on your head? What has happened to you?"

"No man wants a girl who runs away, are you happy with your spinsterhood?"

I smiled and politely answered all their questions. Then I moved right on to stiff awkward conversations with Khoush and Himba elected officials. Nothing was asked of Okwu and Okwu was pleased, preferring to menacingly loom in the background behind me. Okwu was happiest around human beings when it was menacingly looming.

I was exhausted. My temples were throbbing, my mind wanting a moment to focus on what had nearly happened with Okwu right outside the Third Fish and not getting a chance to do so. On top of all this, I still needed days to recover from the stress of traveling through space for the equivalent of three days and then the physical shift of being on Earth. Finally, when it was all done, we were escorted to the special shuttle arranged for Okwu and me. My family was offered a separate shuttle. I was glad for the solitude. As soon as I was inside, I slumped in my seat and tried not to look at Okwu clumsily squeezing and then bumbling into the shuttle that was clearly not made for its kind.

"Your land is dry," Okwu said, turning to the large bulbous window at the back as we bulleted through the desert lands between Kokure and Osemba. "Its life is not water-based."

"There used to be more water here," I said, my eyes closed. "Then the climate changed and it went underground or dried up and the rains fell elsewhere."

"I cannot understand why my people warred with the Khoush," it said and we were quiet for a while. I too had often wondered why the Meduse fought with the Khoush and not some other tribe inhabiting the wetter parts of the world.

"But the Khoush have many lakes," I said. "It's us Himba who live closest to the deep desert, the hinterland. And even in my village, we have a lake. It's pink in the sunlight because of all the salt in it."

"When I see this god body, my people will know."

I'd once asked Okwu about its planet Omuriro and it had said little. It told me there was no water on Omuriro, but everything was soft, fleshy, and connected. "You can't breathe there without a mask, but you would be adored," Okwu had said. The Meduse worshipped water as a god, for they believed they came from it. This was the root of the war between the Meduse and the Khoush, though the details had long been blasted away by violence and death, and then angry, most likely incorrect, tales of heroism or cowardice depending on the teller.

I briefly wondered what would happen if Okwu swam in the lake, since it had never been in a body of water. But I didn't ask.

The Root

My family's house has been called "the Root" for over a hundred and fifty years. It's been in our family for longer than the existence of its name. One of the first homes built in the Himba village of Osemba, the Root was made entirely of stone. Even the bioluminescent plants growing on the outside walls and the roof were generations old. The house was passed down through the women, and my mother—being the oldest daughter in her family and the only one born with the gift of mathematical sight—had been the clear inheritor of it when her mother passed.

A huge edifice built in an upward spiral shape stemming from the enormous meeting room on the bottom floor, the Root also had a spacious kitchen, seven bathrooms, and nine bedrooms. As everything was in Himbaland, the Root was solar powered, its grids so well embedded into the sides and roof of the house that their bases had melted and blended with the stone. The Root was old and more like a self-sustaining creature than a house. My father often joked that one day it would sprout a new bedroom next to mine.

The meeting room was open to all extended family members and close friends whenever they needed it, be it day or night. In this way, home was never a quiet place or a private one. There were no locks on any of the doors, not even in the bathrooms, and mealtimes were always grand occasions. So in many ways, the evening of my homecoming was no different from any other. However, in other ways, it certainly was.

Okwu's arrival in Osemba wasn't as spectacular (or terrifying) as its arrival at the launch port. A modest group of people were there to welcome us and gawk at Okwu, but most would come later in the evening. My family arrived in the shuttle behind us and most of them quickly headed home to get ready for the dinner that night.

"Okwu," my father said in Himba, stepping up to us. He was shakily grinning as he looked up at it. "Welcome, to our village." Okwu just floated there and my father glanced at me, his smile faltering. I motioned for him to keep talking. "Okay, heh, I am amazed by how you stood up to the Khoush. They don't treat us Himba very well, either. But we are a quiet people, so . . . we tolerate it and work with them. Come see what I've made for you."

We followed my father around the house. I let my sandals dig into the warm red dirt as I walked. It was so so good to be home.

"Oh," my father peeped, turning to walk backward as Okwu and I followed. "I *really* enjoy the way you speak our language. Did my daughter teach you?"

"Yes," Okwu said. "She is a good teacher."

"She's a *true* master harmonizer," my father said, turning around.

I bit my lip and said nothing.

When we rounded the corner into the back, I was glad to have something to change the subject. "You can credit me for this," my father said, turning to us with his arms out. Okwu thrummed with pleasure from deep in its dome.

"Oh, Papa," I said, laughing. "This is amazing."

Okwu moved past him to the large transparent tent. It touched the flap and a doorway sized just larger than Okwu's body opened, lavender gas billowing out. Okwu floated inside, the flap closing behind it.

"I'm a master harmonizer too," Papa said, looking at me and winking. "And a good researcher. Once I knew the components, it was easy to build a machine that creates their breathing gas. It's similar to the gas produced in some of the spouts near the Khoushland volcanoes."

"This was all your idea?" I asked, grinning.

"Of course," he said. "The enemy of my enemy is my friend . . . even if it's a monster."

"Okwu isn't a monster, Papa."

"It nearly killed you on that ship and it nearly killed us all at the launch port." When I opened my mouth to protest, he held up a hand. "It's the job of the master harmonizer to make peace and friendship, to harmonize. For you to befriend that thing, you've done well."

I gave him a tight hug. "Thank you."

Okwu didn't come out, except to thank my father and say, "I am very comfortable in here. You are Binti's father."

~

My bedroom was the same as when I'd left it. My table was messy with astrolabe parts, bits of wire, and sandstone dust; my closet was closed and my bed was made. There was a package on my bed wrapped in thin red cloth. I smiled. Only my mother would wrap a gift with such care, and always with red cloth. I turned it over, rubbing a hand across the smooth coolness of it, and set it back on my bed. I'd open it later, when things were quiet.

I went to my travel pod and brought out the dress I'd bought in Oomza Uni on a rare occasion where I'd gone shopping. Long and flowing, its design was vaguely Khoush, but mostly something else, and it was sky blue, a color Himba rarely wore. I put it on. When I came downstairs to join everyone in the meeting room, I immediately regretted wearing it. *Stupid stupid, stupid,* I thought, looking around. *I've been away too long.* Feeling the burn of everyone's stares, I made a beeline for my mother, who'd just gone into the kitchen.

Two of my mother's older sisters stood over a huge pot full of boiling rice and another bubbling with bright yellow curried goat stew. My mother lifted the heavy lid of a pot full of red stew so she could dump in a large plate of roasted chicken wings. My stomach grumbled at the sight of it all. With all the delicious exotic foods I'd eaten and prepared in my dorm kitchen on Oomza Uni, nothing compared to a simple plate of spiced rice and spicy red stew with chicken.

"Mama," I said, keeping my voice down so my aunties wouldn't hear. "When do this season's group of women leave for pilgrimage? I couldn't calculate the time or access news of the leaves from off planet." I chuckled nervously looking at my mother, whose eyebrows rose. The pilgrimage time was calculated through numbers based on the current composition of local clay and written on three large palm tree leaves. These leaves were passed from home to home over a month until all Himba knew.

"*You* want to go on your pilgrimage?" my mother asked.

I nodded. "I want to see everyone, of course, but this is why I came home, too."

My mother and I said it simultaneously, "It's time."

Then we both nodded. She reached out and carefully touched my *okuoko*. She took one in her hand and squeezed it. I winced.

"So they aren't hair anymore," she said.

"No."

I glanced at my aunties' turned backs. I knew they were listening, as they stirred what was in the pots.

"It did this to you?"

"They," I said. "Not Okwu ... I don't think." I paused, remembering the moment when the stinger was plunged into my back as I knelt before the Meduse chief trying to save my life, those Meduse and the lives of so many others on Oomza Uni. "Really, I don't know if it was Okwu; I didn't see."

"They're a hive mind," she said. "So it doesn't matter." She was rubbing the *otjize* off to reveal the true transparent blue of them with darker blue dots on the tips. I held my breath, as she inspected me with a mother's eye and hand. She whispered softly and I held still. My mother only used her mathematical sight to protect the family. Now she used it to look into me. Deep.

She'll see everything, I thought. Seconds passed, her hand grasping my *okuoko*, her eyes boring into me, her lips whispering simple, but intuitively smooth equations that slipped away from my ears like oil from soap. I shifted from one foot to the other and prayed to the

Seven that she wouldn't start calling on Them to "come exorcise her polluted daughter" like some distraught mother in the overly dramatic newsfeed shows my sisters enjoyed watching. Suddenly, my mother let go of my *okuoko* and looked at me with clear eyes. Blinking. She lifted my chin. "The women leave tomorrow."

My eyes grew wide. "Oh no! But . . . but I just got here!"

"Yes. For such a gifted harmonizer, your timing has always been awful."

"My pilgrimage dress. Is that what's in this package?" I asked.

She nodded.

"You knew."

"You're my daughter," my mother said. When she pulled me to her and hugged me tightly, I rested my head on her chest and sighed. "Even if you're wearing these strange blue clothes that make you look like some sort of masquerade."

I burst out laughing.

~

All nine of my siblings came to my welcoming dinner, aunts, uncles, cousins, nieces, and nephews. Chief Kapika of the local Himba Council came too, as did his second-wife Neeka. Only my best friend Dele remained missing. He hadn't been at the launch port, either. I was disappointed, but I would track him down early in the morning, before I left for my four-day pilgrimage.

"What kind of dress is that?" my sister Vera asked, as I stepped from the last stair into the crowded meeting room. "You look like some kind of mermaid masquerade. Maybe you should go greet Mami Wata at the lake." She laughed at her own words.

I prickled. Vera was eleven years older than me, inches taller, and so beautiful that she'd had her pick of husbands from fifteen amazing suitors five years ago. She'd chosen a man who was handsome like a water spirit and an extremely successful astrolabe seller, to my father's delight. Vera was also the most outspoken about my "irresponsibly selfish choice" to leave. She held her two-year-old son on her hip and he looked at me with wide eyes and a precious grin.

"Little Zu seems to like my dress," I said.

"Zu likes anything strange," she said, putting Zu down. He stepped up to me and grasped the bottom of my dress to look at it more closely. "I'm kidding," Vera said. "Honestly, I expected you to come back wearing a skintight spacesuit or something. This isn't so bad. And we're all relieved that you made it home safely."

She gave me a tight hug.

"Thanks," I said.

And that was how the night began. As expected. I had a chance to catch up with several of my age mates, all of whom were proudly betrothed, boys and girls. I was relieved, though slightly bothered, that none of them asked if I were here to enter a betrothal too. Chief Kapika gave a speech about Himba pride. "And now our Binti Ekeopara Zuzu Dambu Kaipka of Osemba is back with us; now the community can contract back into itself like a self-protecting flower. We are all here. And that is good." When he'd finished talking, everyone applauded. I'd smiled, uncomfortably. I was returning to Oomza Uni in two months for the beginning of next quarter, but I didn't have to tell everyone this yet.

Eventually, we all sat down to eat and that's when everything went wrong. I was enjoying a second helping of ostrich stew, my stomach stretched beyond its usual point. Back on Oomza Uni, Professor Okpala demanded that all her mathematics students control their daily intake of rich foods. To be full made treeing more difficult, she'd said. She was right. I'd never been one to eat more than what my body required, but I found my mind was sharper when I stayed just a little hungry with every meal. Over the months, I grew used to this not-quite-full sensation. However, today, I indulged.

I felt slow and heavy. And at the moment, to my delight, I was alone. The better to focus on my food. My father stood a few feet away with his two brothers, Uncle Gideon and Uncle Akpe, talking. One moment, Uncle Gideon was laughing raucously at something and then the next, he was struggling to keep my father from toppling over.

"Papa!" I shrieked, jumping up. It was as if my father's fall created a vacuum, for everyone in the room rushed toward him. My brother Bena got to him before me, pushing me aside to do so.

My mother came running. "Moaoogo," she shouted. "Moaoogo, what is the matter?"

Bena and my uncle held him up. "I'm fine," my father insisted, but he was out of breath. "I'm fine." Even as he spoke, he winced, limply holding his hands together. And it was then that I noticed the joints of his fingers were extremely swollen, almost bulbous. When had my father developed arthritis? I frowned as my sister Vera stepped up beside me on one side, her son clasping her skirts, and my oldest sister Omaihi on the other. I am not short, but all of my sisters, even my younger sister Peraa, who is two years my junior, were taller than me. Between Vera and Omaihi, I felt like a child standing between adult giants.

"Papa are you alright?" my sister Omaihi asked.

"Yes, yes, yes," our father insisted, as his brothers helped him to sit down. My brother Bena joined Vera,

Omaihi, and me, his arms across his chest and a frown on his face.

"Papa's always overdoing it," he said. "Stands all day in the shop working on the astrolabes and then comes to dinner and *still* doesn't sit down."

"Now you see, Binti," Vera hissed.

I could feel them all glaring at me now. "How long has he been—"

"Since you left, really," Vera said, looking squarely at me. Bena and Omaihi looked at me too.

"What?" I asked. "You think I caused it by leaving?"

Vera scoffed and only continued glaring at me.

I looked to Bena and Omaihi for support, but they said nothing.

"That's so wrong," I said.

"It's the truth," Vera said, her voice sharply rising. I looked around. She meant everyone to hear. "Binti, now that you're here, I think you need some tough truth."

"Before you have the nerve to disappear in the night again," Omaihi firmly added.

"I . . . I didn't leave at night, I left in the early morning," I muttered. I took a deep breath, slipped my hand into my front pocket, and grasped my *edan*. It was mine, the object that I was studying at the university over a dozen planets away, a place my sisters, my family, had never set foot on.

Vera stepped closer, leaning in as she looked down her nose at me. Her *otjize*-covered locks nearly reached her knees and they made my *okuoko* look like buds to a tree full of blooming flowers. "See Papa! *You* were supposed to take over the shop, so he could sit down and be proud. We're all very happy to see you, Binti. But you should be ashamed of yourself. Your selfishness nearly got you killed!" Now she was pointing her index finger in my face. I could hear my heart beating in my ears. "Then what would Papa do? And ... and even if you *die*, the world will move on. Who are you? You're not famous."

I was squeezing my *edan,* but somehow, I stayed quiet. The entire room was quiet and listening. Where were my parents? There they were, yards away. My father was sitting now, my mother and uncles beside him. All were just looking at us.

"You'll always be alone if you don't stop this and come home," my oldest sister added. Her voice wasn't as loud as Vera's, but it was much harder. "Jumping back and forth between planets, you have to slow down."

A few people in the room grunted agreement.

"I'm doing what I believe the Seven created me to do!" I said. But my voice was shrill and breathless. I was dizzy from the strain of controlling my outrage, needing to say my piece and feeling that shame that had resided deep within me since I'd left. "Do you even understand what I *did* on that ship? Everyone was *dead,* except the pilot and me! I *saw* them do it! I—"

"Then you befriended the enemy of humanity," my brother Bena said from behind me.

I whirled around and said, "No, the enemy of the Khoush people. You know, the people *you've* been railing against since you learned how to read?" I turned back to Vera, who grandly sucked her teeth, as she looked me up and down with disgust.

"You're so ugly now, Binti," she said. "You don't even sound the same. You're polluted. Almost eighteen years old. What man will marry you? What kind of children will you have now? Your friend Dele doesn't even want to see you!"

That last part was like a snakebite.

"Maybe you shouldn't have come back," Vera growled, her face inches from mine. I could practically feel her keeping herself from punching me in the face. *Do it,* I told her with my eyes. *I dare you.* My cheeks were hot and my body had begun to tremble.

"Some of the girls here now want to do what you did," she said. "You're supposed to be a master harmonizer. Look at you. What harmony do you bring here?"

I tried to grab even the simplest equation, $1 + 1$, $0 + 0$, $5 - 2$, 2×1. I tried to do what I did on that ship, when I held my own life in my hands, when I'd faced a race of people who detested all humans because of a few humans. But every number eluded my mental grasp. All I could see was my sister's *otjize*-covered face with her long silver earrings that clicked to enunciate her words and her elaborate sandstone and gold marriage necklace that meant more to everyone here than my traveling to another planet to be a student at the greatest university in the galaxy.

She stepped even closer. "You bring dissonance! What if . . ."

"Enough!" I screamed at her, shaking with anger. "Who . . . who are you, Vera?" I couldn't find any more words. Instead I inhaled sharply and then did something I'd never thought of doing, even when at my angriest. I spat in her face. It landed on her cheek. Immediately, I regretted my actions. However, instead of shutting up, I continued shouting, "Do you have any clue who I am?" Even as I carried the weight of my regret, it felt wonderful to roar like that at her, at everyone. I was about to say more when Vera shrieked, my saliva still glistening on her face. She scrambled back, falling over a chair. Her elbow knocked over a cup of water on a table, which rolled to the edge and shattered on the floor. I heard my father exclaim. Behind me, I heard Bena gasp and scamper away from me too.

Vera raised her hands, shaking her head, and she whispered, "I'm sorry, I'm sorry, Binti, I'm sorry!"

"Move away from her," I heard one of my uncles say. "Everyone."

"*Kai!*" someone exclaimed. "What is that?"

I saw my four-year-old niece on the other side of the round table drop her drumstick of chicken and bury her face against the leg of my oldest brother, Omeva. He didn't notice her do this because he was staring at me, his mouth agape. People fled the room, covered their eyes, cowered in corners. I met the blank eyes of my mother and held them for a long time and that was when I realized what was happening. My *okuoko*. They were writhing atop my head, again.

"What has happened to my harmonizing daughter?" I heard my father softly ask. "The peacemaker? She spits in her older sister's face." He pressed his right hand to his eyes; the joints were so gnarled.

I let go of the *edan* in my pocket and pressed my hand to my chest. The rage in me retreated. "Papa, I . . ."

"What did that place do to you?" he asked, still covering his face.

I couldn't stop the tears from falling. I didn't *know* what it all had done to me. It was there sometimes, and then sometimes, it wasn't. I was peaceful, then all I could see was war. My siblings had been attacking me. How was peace going to help? I wanted to say these things. I wanted to explain to them all. Instead, I fled the dining room. I left my family to continue talking about me in my absence as they had since I'd left. As I ascended the stairs, I heard them start in. Vera began, then my brothers.

I slammed my bedroom door behind me and just stood there. My entire body was shuddering. I'd traveled so far to come home and rest in the arms of my family and now I'd just cast myself out. "Even a masquerade has its people, only a ghost wanders alone," my father liked to say. *I have to fix this,* I desperately thought. But my mind was too full of adrenaline and fury to think of anything.

The gift on my bed caught my eye. I unwrapped it and unfolded the silky wrapper, matching top and veil inside it, all the deep orange color of *otjize*. "Beautiful," I whispered. Lovely light weather-treated material that would make walking in the desert under the noon sun like standing in the shade. A girl's or woman's pilgrimage clothes were the most expensive and treasured clothes she would have until her wedding day.

I laughed bitterly. These would probably be the most expensive and treasured clothes in my life. "No marriage for me," I muttered. My words made me snicker to myself and then I laughed harder. Soon, I was laughing so hard that my belly muscles were cramping.

When I calmed down, I listened, still hearing my family talking loudly in the meeting room. I shook out my pilgrimage clothes and laid them on my chair. I brought out my astrolabe and *edan* and placed them side by side on my bed. I shut my eyes and was about to do one of the breathing exercises Professor Okpala had taught me when my astrolabe chimed. Someone was trying to reach me. I paused, my eyes closed, going through a list of who it could possibly be.

My sisters? Probably.

My father? No.

My mother? Possibly.

My uncles or aunties? Likely.

I opened my eyes and saw Dele's face filling in the circular screen of my astrolabe. He was looking down at his hands, as he waited for me to accept his call. "Dele," I said and the notification chimes stopped. He looked up, seeing me, and we stared at each other. We hadn't spoken since I left. He wouldn't answer or return my calls and he had never called me. He looked older, now . . . and wiser.

"You have a beard," I blurted. It was light and fuzzy, but a beard it was.

"I've joined the Himba Council." He didn't smile as he conveyed this news. Then he just stared at me. I stared back. The Himba Council? Was he next in line to apprentice for Council Chief? Dele? Council apprentices weren't allowed to leave Himbaland. When had Dele become so . . . rooted? From downstairs, they still talked, voices raised. Now, I heard my mother speaking. Shouting?

"How have you been?" I finally asked.

"Here," he said.

More silence. "What . . . what do you want, Dele?"

"Your sister messaged me to call you immediately," he said. "What's going on?"

"*This* is why you finally reach out to me?"

"You were the one who left, not me."

"So?"

Silence.

"Dele . . . I couldn't tell you," I said. "Everyone . . . *you* just assumed I wasn't going, that I wasn't *supposed* to go. I *wanted* to, Dele. So badly. Haven't you ever wanted something with all your heart, yet . . ."

"Yet, not one person in my family, in my entire *clan*, wanted it for me? No, Binti, never. That would be selfish. I'm not Khoush."

Dele and I had known each other since we were babies and as we grew older, Dele had begun to lean more and more toward embracing the deep Himba way. We used to joke and argue about it, but our friendship always won out over the laws, rules, and mores. Plus, back then, his traditional leanings made him seem so strong and important, despite my dislike of it. Now, he'd grown a beard.

"You're too complex, Binti," he said. "That's why I

stayed away. You're my best friend. You are. And I miss you. But, you're too complex. And look at you; you're even stranger now." He pointed into the camera. "You think you can cover those things with *otjize* and I won't see them? I know you."

I sat down hard on my bed, feeling breathless again. Had my sister told him about my *okuoko*? Could he really see them through the camera? They weren't even moving.

"What are you trying to accomplish with all this?" he asked. "I can see it in your face, you're not well. You look tired and sad and . . ."

"Because of what just happened!" I said. "Why don't you ask me about that? Instead of assuming the greatest choice I've ever made for myself is making me sick? *Home* is making me sick! I was fine until I got here." This wasn't all true, of course, but I needed to make my point clearly.

"We all love you," he said. "You don't know how your leaving made your family suffer. Your father's business may have increased because of you, but his health has decreased. That doesn't bode well for our village. He's more our leader than our *chief*! He's master harmonizer! And people here . . . ask your younger sister, girl cousins how they get treated. You've stained them. Marriage won't be . . ."

"None of that's my fault!"

Dele paused and shook his head, chuckling softly. Then, again, we were staring at each other.

He waved a hand at me. "I can't help you, Binti."

"Can't help you, either," I snapped.

"I hear you're going on pilgrimage tomorrow," he said. "You have strange timing, but good luck."

"Thanks," I said, looking away.

"I trust you will take care of yourself," he said, coolly. Then Dele was gone. And for the first time, it really sunk in. No man wanted a girl who ran away. No man would marry me.

I pushed my astrolabe and *edan* aside, lay on my bed, curled up, and cried myself to sleep.

Night Masquerade

I awoke hours later with a face crusty with tears, dried *otjize*, and snot. I went to the bathroom, blew and wiped my nose, and looked at myself in the mirror. Old *otjize* was flaking from my cheeks and forehead, leaving patches of clear brown bare skin. I needed to remove it all and reapply. I'd feel more myself, I knew. I didn't pause on the knowledge that my current batch of *otjize* was made with clay from another planet. As I stared at my haggard face in the mirror, I glanced at the window facing the back of the house and remembered Okwu was out there.

I tiptoed downstairs and peeked into the main room. There were a few still awake, softly chatting in a corner, my sister Vera one of them. Many were curled up on flat pillows and mats. I snuck out the back door and nearly walked right into Okwu.

"It didn't go well," it said.

"No," I said, stepping around it to go look at its gas-filled tent. The tent's tall puffy girth reminded me of a giant Meduse. Maybe that's what my father was going for when he set it up.

"Your father came out to check on me," Okwu said. "He seemed upset."

I grunted, but said nothing more of it. "Do you want to go see the lake?" I said.

Okwu puffed out a great amount of gas and I coughed, fanning the air around me. "Yes," it said, its voice so clear that the vibration of it made my head ache.

My home village Osemba was a palette of dusty browns from the dirt roads to stone and sand-brick buildings. The oldest buildings were groupings of several solid stone structures, like the Root with its many traditional conical roofs. The Root sits at the very edge of Osemba. About a mile west, the sand dunes begin threatening to reclaim the clay-rich land. In the opposite direction, straight down the main dirt road, past other homes and a small area reserved for the western morning souq, is the lake. The rest of Osemba spreads along the lake's edges.

Okwu and I walked up the road in the dark of deep night. We, Himba, are a people of the sun. When it sets, we retreat. The night is typically for sleep, family, and reflection. Thus, Okwu and I had the road to ourselves and I was glad. I used my astrolabe to light our way. I glanced at Okwu every so often and noted how as it floated beside me, it turned this way and that, observing Osemba; the first Meduse to ever do this, in peace or war.

"I can smell the water," Okwu said, minutes later.

"It's right in front of us," I said. "Those tables and wooden medians are for the souq that's here every morning; it's similar to the marketplace on Oomza, but with just humans, of course."

"Then that's not like Oomza Blue Market at all," Okwu said.

"No, the setup. People sell things outside. Come, the lake is just past it."

"How can the air smell of water?" Okwu asked in Otji-himba. The awe it felt was clearer when it spoke in my language. I smiled and walked faster, enjoying Okwu's rare excitement.

When I stepped onto the sand, Okwu beside me, I quickly took a deep breath and held it. *Phoom.* Okwu's gas plumed so thickly around me that for a moment all I saw was the line of my astrolabe's light tinted lavender. I took several steps from Okwu, fanning the gas away until I reached breathable space. Still, I coughed, laughing as I did. "Okwu," I gasped. "Calm down—"

But Okwu wasn't there. I quickly flashed my astrolabe's light around me and noticed two things at once. The first was that Okwu was floating to the water, moving swiftly as if blown by a strong wind. The second was that I didn't need my light to see this because the light from the lake was more than enough. *Light from the water,* I slowly thought as another thought competed for my attention. *Can Okwu even swim? Salt is in water, too.*

"Okwu," I shouted, running toward the water.

But Okwu floated into its waters and quickly sunk in. Then it was gone. I splashed in all the way to my knees, the warm buoyancy of the water already feeling as if it wanted to lift me up. "Okwu?" I shouted. Around me was blinking electric green light. It was clusterwink snail season and the water was full of the spawning bioluminescent baby snails, the tiny creatures each flashing their own signals of whatever they were signaling. It was like wading into an overpopulated galaxy.

I waded farther into the water looking for Okwu. I paused, wondering if I should dive in to search for it. I couldn't swim, but because of the high salt content, I couldn't drown; the water would just push me to the surface. Still, if I went after Okwu, the water would wash off my *otjize*. And if anyone saw me, if my people didn't think I was crazy yet, they certainly would after word spread that I'd been outside *otjize*-free.

"Okwu?" I shouted one last time. *What if the water just dissolved its body?* I looked at the glowing water and braced my legs to throw myself farther in and paddle out to find Okwu. Then yards into the water, within the twinkling green stars, I saw a swirling galaxy. Okwu's silhouette surrounded by swirling twinkling baby snails. "What?" I whispered.

Then Okwu's dome emerged; Okwu was adeptly swimming, half-submerged. It came toward me, but stopped when the water got too shallow for it to stay half-submerged. "My ancestors are dancing," Okwu said in Otjihimba, its voice wavering with more emotion than I'd ever heard Okwu convey. Then Okwu swam back into the water. For the next thirty minutes, it danced with the snails.

I sat on the beach, my long skirts covering my *otjize*-free legs, in the twinkling green of my home lake. Traditionally, it's taboo for a Himba woman or girl to bathe with water, let alone openly swim in the lake. I'd developed a love for bathing with water in the dorms on Oomza Uni. Though I'd only do it when I was relatively sure no one was around. As I sat there, watching Okwu dance with its god, I thought about how strange it was that for me to swim in water was taboo and for Okwu such a taboo was itself a taboo.

I remember thinking, *The gods are many things.*

~

I don't know why I was doing it.

Even after seeing Okwu dancing with its god, some of the fury and pain from my dinner with family still coursed through my system. So an hour later, there I sat on my bedroom floor working my fingers over my *edan*'s lines as I hummed to it as Professor Okpala had taught me—mathematical harmonizing plus the soft vibration waves from my voice sometimes reached normally unreachable sensors on some *edans*.

My window was open and outside a cool desert breeze was blowing in from the west, pushing my orange curtains inward. The current of the breeze disturbed the mathematical current I was calling up. The disturbance caused my mind to weave in a tumble of equations that strengthened what I was trying to do instead of weaken it.

As I hummed, I let myself tree, floating on a bed of numbers soft, buoyant, and calm like the lake water. *Just beautiful,* I thought, feeling both vague and distant and close and controlled. My hands worked and soon I slid a finger on one of the triangular sides of the *edan*. It slid open and then slipped off. Inside the pyramid point was another wall of metal decorated with a different set of geometric swirls and loops. Professor Okpala described it as "another language beneath the language." My *edan* was all about communication, one layer on top of another and the way they were arranged was another language. I was learning, but would I ever master it?

"Ah," I sighed. Then I slipped the other triangular side

of the pyramid off and the current I called caught both and lifted them into the air before my eyes. "Bring it up," I whispered and the *edan* joined the two metal triangles. They began to slowly rotate in the way they always did, the *edan* like a small planet and the triangles like flat cartwheeling moons. A small yellow moth that had been fluttering about my room attracted to the *edan*'s glow flew to it now and was instantly caught up in the rotating air.

Was it the presence of the moth, tumbling and fluttering between the metal triangles? I do not know. There was always so much I didn't know, but not knowing was part of it all. Whatever the reason, suddenly my *edan* was shedding more triangle sides from its various pyramid points and they joined the rotation. What remained of my *edan* hovered in the center and from the cavernous serenity of meditation, I sighed in awe. It was a gold metal ball etched with deep lines that formed many wild loops that did not touch, reminiscent of fingerprint patterns. Was it solid gold? Gold was a wonderful conductor; imagine how precise the current I guided into it would move. If I did that, would the sphere open too? Or even . . . speak?

The moth managed to break out of the cycle and as soon as it did, my grasp slipped. As Professor Okpala would have said, I fell out of the tree. The mathematical current I'd called up evaporated and all the pieces of my *edan* fell to the floor, musically clinking. I gasped and stared. I waited for several moments and nothing happened. Always, the pieces rearranged themselves back into my *edan,* as if magnetized, even when I fell out of the tree.

"No, no, no!" I said, gathering the pieces and putting them in a pile in the center of my bed. I waited, again. Nothing. "Ah!" I shrieked, near panic. I snatched up the gold ball. So heavy. Yes, it had to be solid gold. I brought it to my face, my hands shaking and my heart pounding. I rubbed the pad of my thumb over the deep labyrinthine configurations. It was warm and heavier than the *edan* had ever felt, as if it had its own type of gravity now that it was exposed.

I was about to call up another current to try to put it back together when something outside caught my eye. I went to my window and what I saw made my skin prickle and my ears ring. I stumbled back, ran my finger over the *otjize* on my skin, and rubbed it over my eyelids to ward off evil. My bedroom was at the top floor of the Root and it faced the west where my brother's garden grew, the backyard ended, and the desert began.

"May the Seven protect me," I whispered. "I am not supposed to be seeing this." No girl or woman was. And even though I never had up until this point, I knew exactly who that was standing in my brother's garden in the dark, looking right at me, *pointing* a long sticklike finger at me. I shrieked, ran to my bed, and stared at my disassembled *edan*. "What do I do, what do I do? What's happening? What do I do?"

I slowly stepped back to the window. The Night Masquerade was still there, a tall mass of dried sticks, raffia, and leaves with a wooden face dominated by a large tooth-filled mouth and bulbous black eyes. Long streams of raffia hung from its round chin and the sides of the head, like a wizard's beard. Thick white smoke flowed out from the top of its head and already I could smell the smoke in my room, dry and acrid. Okwu's tent was several yards to the right, but Okwu must have been inside.

"Binti," I heard the Night Masquerade growl. "Girl. Small girl from big space."

I moaned, breathless with terror. My oldest brother, father, and grandfather had seen the Night Masquerade at different times in their lives. My father on the night he became the family master harmonizer over two decades ago. My oldest brother on the night he'd fought three Khoush men in the street outside the market when they'd wrongfully accused him of stealing the fine astrolabes he'd brought to sell. And my grandfather, when he was eight years old on the night after he saved his whole village during a Khoush raid by hacking the astrolabes of the Khoush soldiers to produce an eardrum-rupturing sound. Only men and boys were said to even have the ability to *see* the Night Masquerade and only those who were heroes of Himba families got to see it. No one ever spoke of what happened after seeing it. I'd never considered it. I'd never needed to.

I ran to my travel pod and pulled out a small sealed sack I'd used to store tiny crystal snail shells I'd found in the forest near my dorm on Oomza Uni. I dumped them onto my bed, where they crackled and began to turn from white to yellow as they reacted to the dry desert air. I bristled with annoyance. I'd brought the shells to show my sisters and now they'd be dust in a few minutes.

I pushed them aside and put the pieces of my *edan* into the transparent sack, wincing at their clinking and clattering. The gold sphere with its fingerprint-like ridges was still warm. I paused for a moment, holding it. Would it melt or burn the sack? I put it inside; the sack was made from the stomach lining of a creature whose powerful stomach juices could digest the most complex metals and stones on the planet. If it could withstand that, it certainly could contain my *edan*'s warm core.

I'd just put the sack into my satchel when there came a hard knock at my door. I twitched as the noise sent me back to the ship when the Meduse had knocked so hard on my door. I covered my mouth to hold in the scream that wanted to escape, then I shut my eyes. I took a deep lung-filling breath and let it out. Inhaled again. Exhaled. *No Meduse at the door, Binti,* I thought. *Okwu is outside and it is your friend.* The knock came again, followed by my father's voice calling my name. I ran to the door and opened it and met his frowning eyes. Behind him stood my older brother Bena, also frowning.

"Did you see it?" my father asked.

I nodded.

"*Kai!*" Bena exclaimed, pressing his hands to his closely shaven head. "How is this possible?"

"I don't know!" I said, tears welling in my eyes.

"What is it?" my mother asked, coming up behind him, rubbing her face. The *otjize* on her skin was barely a film. Normally only my father would see her like this.

My younger sister Peraa peeked from the staircase. She was the eyes of my family, silent and curious about all things. *Had she seen it, too?* I wondered.

Somehow, my father knew she was there, and he whipped around to shout, "Peraa, go back to bed!"

"Papa, there are people outside," she said.

"People?" Bena asked. "Peraa, did you see anything else?"

Before she could respond, my father asked, "What people?"

"Many people," Peraa said. She was out of breath and looked about to cry. "Desert People!"

"Eh?!" my father exclaimed. "What is happening tonight?" Then he was storming down the hall to the stairs, my brother rushing after him.

"Wait," my mother said, holding a hand up to me. "Go in, apply *otjize*. Put on your pilgrimage attire."

"Why? That's not for . . ."

"Do it."

Peraa was still standing at the top of the staircase, staring at me. I motioned for her to come, but she only shook her head and went downstairs.

My mother's eyes migrated to my *otjize*-rolled *okuoko*.

"Do those hurt?" she asked.

"Only if you hurt them."

"Why'd you have to do it?"

"Mama, would you rather I died like everyone else on that ship?"

"Of course not," she said. She seemed about to say more, but instead she just said, "Hurry." Then she turned and quickly headed down the staircase.

~

I applied my *otjize* and put on my pilgrimage clothes. The *otjize* would rub off onto my clothes making tonight the outfit's official event, not my pilgrimage, blessed on this day by my *otjize*. *So be it,* I thought. Before I went out to the front door, I snuck to the back of the house. Okwu was waiting for me. "There are people standing around your home," it said in Meduse.

"I know." I resisted staring at the desert woman yards away watching us. Tall with dark brown skin that looked so strange to my eyes because she wore no *otjize*, she looked a few years older than I, possibly in her early twenties. Her bushy hair was a sweet black and it shivered in the breeze.

"I watched them arrive," Okwu said. "One asked me to come out of my tent. When I did, he spoke to me in Meduse. How do people who live far from water know our language?"

"I don't know," I said. "Did . . . did you see anything near the house? Standing where my window faces?"

"No."

"Okay," I muttered, turning from it. "Hold on. I need to see something." The desert woman watched me as I slowly walked to the spot where the Night Masquerade had been. "I'm just checking something," I said to her.

"Even if you ran, I'd catch you," she said in Otjihimba, with a smirk. "You're why we're here." She motioned to Okwu. "And to see that one."

"Why? What did we do?"

She only chuckled, waving a hand dismissively at me. I stopped at the spot where I was sure the Night Masquerade had been. The sand here was undisturbed, not even a light footprint. It was breezy tonight, but not so much that footprints would disappear in minutes.

"Binti," I heard my mother call.

"Okwu, meet me in the front," I said.

"Okay."

I turned and headed back into the Root.

Blood

The Desert People surrounded the Root the way groups of lake crabs surround their egg-filled holes when the eggs are ready to hatch. There were about seven of them that I could see, probably more on the other side of the house. Some were men, some were women, and all had skin that was "old African" dark, like my father's and mine. They wore the traditional goat-pelt wraps around their waists, blue waist beads, and blue tops. Around their wrists, they wore bracelets made from shards and chunks of pink salt found in dried lakes deep in the desert. None of them wore shoes.

Straight backed, faces stern, they stood silent. Waiting. And though it was very late in the night, a few neighbors had come out to see what was going on. Of course. By sunup, the village's bush radio would carry the word to all of Osemba that Desert People had come to the Root. Khoush communities in Kokure might even hear about it. I felt Okwu's presence not far behind me as it came round the house. I turned and nodded at it.

My father was speaking with a tall old woman. Behind

her stood two camels with packs on their backs. I watched for a moment, as the woman's hands worked wildly while she spoke. Sometimes, she'd stop speaking entirely yet her hands would keep going, moving in circles, jabbing, zigzagging, sometimes harshly, other times gently. This was the way of the Desert People, one of the reasons the Himba viewed them as primitive and mentally unstable. They had no control of their hands; the elders said it was some sort of neurological condition. When the old woman saw me, she smiled and then told my father, "We'll bring her back by tomorrow night."

My mouth fell open and I looked at my father, who did not look at me.

"How will I know?" my father asked.

She looked down her nose at him. "Such a proud son you are."

My father finally looked at me. My mother grabbed my hand. "Not going anywhere," she muttered. I was shocked by so much that I could only stare at her. "We just got her back!" my mother told my father.

"You people are so brilliant, but your world is too small," the old woman who was my father's mother, my *grandmother,* said. "One of you finally somehow grows beyond your cultural cage and you try to chop her stem. Fascinating." She looked at my father. "Don't you remember what happened with your father?" She straightened up. "Your daughter, *my* granddaughter, has seen the Night Masquerade."

My sister Peraa, who was standing beside me now, gasped and looked at me. "You did?" she whispered.

I nodded at her, still unable to speak.

She grabbed my other hand. "Is that why you—"

"No, she hasn't!" my mother snapped.

The old woman chuckled and her hands twitched and began to move again, zigzagging, punching, waving. The astrolabe around her neck bumped against her chest, not once touched by the woman. "Why do you think we came out here? There are rituals to be performed."

Even from where I stood, I could see that her astrolabe was one that had been made by my father. The unique slightly oval shape, the rose-tinted sandstone, this was an astrolabe he'd made some time ago. My mother must have noticed this too, because she turned and gave him a dirty look.

The other Desert People standing close by all laughed, some of them making the strange hand motions. I looked back at Okwu and frowned. Several of my relatives had now gathered, none of whom wanted to stand near Okwu. It stood behind them all, but beside it stood one of the Desert People, a bushy-haired boy of about my age.

"We'll take your daughter, *our* daughter, into the desert," my grandmother said. She turned to Okwu.

"Your daughter, too. She will speak with our clan priest-ess, the Ariya. We bring her back the night after this one."

~

My mother wept and my father had to pry my hand from hers. Seeing her weep made me start to weep. Then Peraa started weeping. My brothers just stood there and I saw my sister Vera angrily walk away. More neighbors came out and there was self-righteous nodding and some mumbling about me bringing the outside to the inside. I heard a gravelly voiced friend of my mother's loudly say, "She should have stayed there."

Okwu said nothing. Nothing at all.

Hinterland

I was walking into the desert with the Desert People.

I turned back to the Root, my legs still moving me up the sand dune. I could still see my brother's garden, my bedroom window, and even the spot below where the Night Masquerade had stood. Then we were moving down the sand dune and I looked back until I couldn't see the Root any longer. "What am I doing?" I whispered.

My grandmother was walking beside me, tall and lean as a tree. "Did you bring *otjize* in your satchel?" she asked.

"Yes," I quietly said, patting my satchel.

She laughed loudly. "Of course you did." She moved her hands in front of her face, smiling, and I frowned, watching her. She said nothing when we were walking up the second sand dune and I took out the jar and began to reapply it to my arms and face, the places my mother had held me and tears had run.

Contrary to what my family thought, I knew exactly who I was going to see and I needed to look my best when I saw her. I had been eight years old and terrified when I met the Ariya completely by chance. She was the first person to whom I'd shown my *edan,* even before my father. She hadn't called it an *edan,* she'd called it a "god stone" and said I was lucky to have it. And now I was being brought to her with the thing in pieces.

~

There were dangerous creatures in the hinterland, and at night many didn't sleep.

A lean boy about my age and height named Mwinyi was charged with protecting the group. He was the one whom I'd glimpsed standing beside Okwu. Unlike the others who had dark-brown hair like me, Mwinyi had a head of bushy red-brown hair and I couldn't tell if the color was due to his hair being full of the desert's red dust or if this was its natural color. And he had a thick matted braid growing in the middle that was so long it reached his knees. It swung about his back like a snake when he walked. I couldn't understand how this boy was going to protect a group of nineteen adults until I saw what he could do.

Three hours after we'd scaled that first sand dune, the pack of wild dogs came. There were at least thirty and you could hear them coming from far away. They yipped and barked with the confidence of a pack that didn't need stealth to catch food or stay safe. They spotted and came at us without hesitation. Only I was terrified. Everyone else simply stopped and sat down on the sand, including the two camels. My grandmother put her hand on my shoulder to keep me calm. "Shhh," she said.

Mwinyi was the only one standing. Then he walked right to the dog pack, his hands moving in the Desert People way. Not slowly. Not quickly. In the soft moonlight, the sight was mystical, like watching something right out of the stories my father liked to tell during the Moon Fest. I couldn't hear him clearly, but I heard him speaking the language of the Desert People. He laughed as the dogs crowded him, sniffing and circling. Then Mwinyi said something and every single one of them stopped moving. And they were looking at him, at his face, as he spoke softly to them.

Then, just as suddenly, every single dog looked at *us*. I gasped and pressed my hands to my gaping mouth. I softly spoke a few choice equations and dropped a degree into meditation, just enough to stop shaking. I wanted to *see* this with all my senses and emotions sharp. Mwinyi was speaking to the dogs who would have harmed us. Several of the dogs near the back yipped agreeably, took one more look at us, and then went on their way. The others followed after a moment.

"He's a harmonizer?" I asked.

My grandmother looked at me. "We don't call them that."

"Then what do you call him?"

"Our son," she said, standing up. Mwinyi waved at us and we continued on our way. As we walked, I reached my hand into my pocket and touched the pouch full of my dissembled *edan*. Even in pieces, it was as much of a mystery to me now as it was when I'd found it . . .

Destiny Is a Delicate Dance

. . . nine years ago. I was out there that morning because I'd grown profoundly angry and run away from home. No one knew that I was angry and no one realized I'd run away. What had upset me was so trivial to my parents and older siblings that they didn't even realize I was up-set. There was to be a dance at the Annual Wind Fest and though all of my age mates were participating, my parents and older siblings had decided it was best for me not to take part in it.

The Diviner had officially tapped me as the next family master harmonizer the week before and so much had al-ready changed about how I was treated and what I was al-lowed and not allowed to do. Now this, all because I had to "sharpen my meditating skills and equation control" when I was already able to tree faster than my father.

Nevertheless, one does not argue with elders. Thus, I had accepted the restriction quietly as I had accepted being tapped as the next master harmonizer, despite the fact that I could never own the shop because I was a fe-male. Shop ownership was my brother's honor. For our family to prove that it could produce a next generation of harmony brought fortune and great respect to us, so I was proud.

But I wanted to dance. I loved dancing. Dancing was like moving my body in the way that I saw numbers and equations move when I treed. When I danced, I could manifest mathematical current within me, harmonizing it with my muscles, skin, sinew, and bones. And now the opportunity had been snatched from me for no other reason besides, "It's just not for you." So I woke up that next morning, dressed in my weather-treated wrapper and top, wrapped my *otjize*-rolled locks in my red veil, quietly packed a satchel, and walked out of the house into the desert before anyone got up.

The desert wasn't a mystery to me. I wasn't supposed to, but I went into it quite often. Sometimes, I went to play, other times I went to find peace and quiet so I could practice treeing. The desert was largely responsible for why I'd gotten so good at treeing so young.

If my family had known that I went out there regularly, instead of going to the lake like all the other children, I'd have been punished with more than a beating. I was smart and stealthy even back then. That early morning, I tiptoed into my parents' room and told them I was go-ing to sit by the lake and watch the early crabs run about. Then I went outside and instead of going toward the lake,

I went the other way, into the desert.

I liked the desert in the morning because it was still cool and it was still. I could go out there and my mind would clear like the sky after a violent power-outing thunderstorm. I would rub an extra-thick layer of *otjize* on my skin and go out sometimes as far as five miles. My astrolabe would start beeping and threatening to alert my parents about my whereabouts if I went any further. I'd see nothing around me but sand, not even the tops of the tallest Osemba buildings, which weren't very tall anyway.

In my childish anger, I was never going to return home. In my mind, I was becoming a nomad, wandering in the desert and letting the sand and wind take me where it would. And as I walked, sometimes, I would dance as I hummed to myself. My feet took me on a two-hour walk north, past the dried cluster of palm trees visible from my bedroom, the patch of hardpan where I'd once found an old seashell, to a place I'd discovered months ago, where a group of gray stones jutted out of the ground like flattened old teeth.

The stones were large enough to sit on and arranged in a wide semicircle that opened west. I'd never asked my parents or schoolteachers about them because then I'd have to tell them where I saw such a thing. I came here often. Sometimes, I brought my small tent, set it up in the middle of the semicircle, and sat inside it while gazing out at the desert as I practiced equations, algorithms, and formulas for mathematical currents that I'd use in astrolabes I was making.

I'd needed the hard silence of the desert because I was still learning back then. This place was perfect. When I practiced, I liked to dig my fingers in the sand and scratch circles, squares, trapezoids, fractals, whatever shapes I needed to visualize the equation. This day when I was eight years old and had run away, I'd set up my tent beside the furthest stone and my fingers drew circles upon circles.

My eyes were half-closed as I watched swirls of sand tumble down a nearby dune. I was whispering a current into being as dividing numbers tumbled through my head. I worked hard not to think about the self-righteous look on my oldest sister's face as she said, "It's just dancing. You have to start sacrificing things like that now."

I was angrily digging my left index finger hard in the sand when I felt it. My nail grazed over it first and I noticed, but unconsciously. I was seeing a short hazy blue line dance before me. Tears fell from my eyes. My family was right. For three years they'd been pushing and pushing me, my mother, father, sisters, brothers, aunts, and uncles. They were all so sure of what I was, that I had the gift. I did have it and now everything was changing because of it. But I just wanted to dance.

The current whirled itself into a perfect circle. Now it was a connection. This would have powered an astrolabe if I had it assembled and positioned for "turn on." I felt a sting and hissed with pain. My hand. My finger. The blue disappeared as I brought my finger to my face for a closer look, my heart slamming in my chest. A scorpion bite all the way out here in the desert, while alone, was very bad news.

My thumb dripped blood and sand was ground into the wound. A tiny gray point poked from the spot where I'd been making circles with my fingers and thumb. Beside it was a small yellow flower. *How'd I miss that?* I wondered. I tried to pick the flower and realized that it was attached to a thin dry but strong white root that clung to whatever was poking from the sand. I put the flower down and grasped the point. It wouldn't budge. I shifted to my knees and leaned closer for a better look.

"Oh," I whispered. "It's not just . . ." I sucked on my finger as I looked at it. Then I started digging around it with my other hand. Soon I was using both hands, disregarding the stinging and light bleeding. Whenever my father allowed me to buy a new book, I spent hours in my room with my eyes closed as I listened to it on my astrolabe. In many of those stories, a curious person would find a secret or magical object that would change her or his life. I'd always wanted that to happen to me. And now I was sure this was it.

This was the Book of Shadows that appeared on the boy's astrolabe when he passed too close to a tree that had just been struck by lightning. This was the jeweled eagle figurine that the girl bought in the market that caused all the birds to come. This was the plant that began to grow in the old man's bedroom after a strange dust storm.

The thing I dug up was a stellated cube. It fit into the palm of my hand and was made of a tarnished metal. There were intricate designs all over it, adept loops and swirls and spirals whose lines never touched each other. I turned it over this way and that, marveling at its complex pointy shape.

"What *is* this thing?" I whispered, awed.

I knocked off the remaining sand and used some of my *otjize* to polish it. This worked better than I expected, for soon its tarnished appearance changed to one of amazing shine. And each time I moved it, it produced a . . . a soft sound. Like the low husky voice of a woman. It was a little scary . . . and fascinating. There was somehow old *current* in this thing. Nevertheless, the more I moved it, the softer the sound until it stopped all together.

Father's eyes will bug out when I show this thing to him, I excitedly thought. And that was how I decided that I was not running away after all. I couldn't wait to hear what he had to say about the mystery device I'd found. Or if he could tell me the best way to study it. *Maybe I can get it to do whatever it was made to do,* I thought. I giggled to myself, sitting on one of the stones and holding the strange thing to my face.

When someone tapped my shoulder, I nearly screamed. And when I whipped around and saw the tall dark-skinned woman with a corona of black hair so huge that it blocked out the sun shining behind her, I did scream. I jumped to my feet and nearly fell over my satchel.

She was one of the Desert People. She looked ten feet tall and everything about her, from her hair to the light sheer blue cloth wrapped around her head to her flowing pants and top made of the same blue material, was blowing in the soft breeze. Slung over her shoulder was a small capture station, its catch bag, and a blue old-looking backpack. I squinted up at her in the sunshine. She was so very tall and so . . . blue. The tallest person I'd ever seen. And somewhat old like my mother's mother. She grasped a thick gnarled walking staff with her long-fingered hands, but she wasn't leaning on it.

"What are you doing out here?" she asked. Her voice was dry and commanding, also like my grandmother, and I immediately stood up straighter.

"I . . . this . . . this is where I . . . please . . . my . . ."

"Oh, shut up, child," she sighed. "Forget I asked." She

rested her staff on her side and began doing that which I'd heard the Desert People did; she moved her hands this way and that, like a child swatting at a fly. I took the moment to quickly look around. There were no others. Could I outrun her? The woman wore no shoes. *How can she stand the hot sand?*

"Binti," she said. "Daughter of Moaoogo Dambu Kaipka Okechukwu Enyi Zinariya."

"That's my name, my father... how do you know?" I whispered. I'd decided that there was no way I could out-run the woman. She was old and carried a staff, but something told me she was strong like a man and she didn't use that staff for walking.

"Do you know who I am?" she asked.

"A desert person?"

She nodded, working her hands before her. It was as if they weren't even part of her body. In my pocket, my as-trolabe buzzed. The sun had just reached its highest peak and it was best to sit in the shade for the next hour. I reached into my pocket to stop it from buzzing.

"I journeyed all the way to this place so I can think," the woman said.

"I... I did, too," I said.

And for a moment, we stared at each other.

"I've been coming here since before your mother was a thought in your grandmother's womb," she said, with a chuckle. "What is that you've found?"

I grasped it more tightly and took a step back. "Nothing. A pretty chunk of . . . metal." I felt sweat prickle in my armpits. To lie to an elder is a sin.

"Don't worry," she said. "I'm not going to take it from you."

"I . . . I never said that," I said.

"I know your grandmother, Binti."

I nearly dropped the *edan* when I looked at her with surprise . . . and understanding. My father's mother was a desert woman and he never spoke of her. Himba men did not wear *otjize,* but sometimes they used it to palm roll or flatten their hair. My father used it to flatten his coarse bushy hair, to mask it. And like me, he was the shade of brown like the Desert People and he'd never liked this fact. My mother was a medium brown, like most Himba, and I knew that he was proud that all their other children were too . . . and that the one who got the desert complexion and hair made up for it by being a master harmonizer.

I'd once asked my father about the Desert People when I was about five years old and he'd snapped at me to never speak of it again. As I looked at this tall woman now, I wanted to go home. I *needed* to go home. My father would kill me for speaking to this woman. I wasn't supposed to be out here in the first place, so meeting her was entirely my fault.

"Do you know what that is you've found?"

I shook my head.

"It's a piece of time from before our time. An ancient work of art and use. It's old, but old doesn't always mean less advanced."

I opened my hand and looked at it. It rested in my palm, comfortable there, but so strange.

"Want to know how to use it?"

I shook my head. "I have to get home," I said. "My father has work for me to finish later today."

"Yes, your gifted father who is so proud of himself." She paused looking me over and then said, "The thing you have, the Himba will call it an *edan,* but we call it a god stone. You're blessed it's found you." She did a few hand motions and laughed. "When you are ready to know how to really use it, find us."

"Okay," I said, smiling the most false smile I had ever smiled. My legs were shaking so vigorously that I felt I would fall to my knees.

"Safe journey home," she said. Then she knelt, touched the sand, and said, "Praise the Seven."

I stood there for a moment surprised, thinking, *Desert People believed in the presence of the Seven, too?* I wondered what my mother would say to this fact, since she thought Desert People were so uncivilized. Not that I'd ever tell her about meeting this woman.

I swiped *otjize* from my face and did the same. Then I turned and ran off. I didn't look back until I was about to crest the first sand dune. She still stood there, beside the gray stones where I'd found the *edan*. I wondered what she'd make of the plant growing there.

~

Early crabs were sneaky and quick, so my parents weren't surprised when I returned empty-handed. I was no longer that angry with my parents, so when I took the *edan* to my father two days later, I didn't have to stifle my emotions. I didn't tell him about the plant growing on it or where I found it. It's the only time I'd lied to my father. I told him I'd bought the thing at the market from a junk seller.

"Who was selling it? Which junk man?" my father anxiously asked. "I need to talk to him! Look at this thing it's—"

"I don't know, Papa," I quickly said. "I wasn't really paying attention. I was so focused on it."

"I'll go to the market tomorrow," my father said, pulling at his scruffy beard. "Maybe someone will have another." He took it from me, his eyes wide. "Beautiful work."

"I think it does something that—"

"The metal," he whispered, staring at the object. He looked at me, smiled and apologetically patted my head. "Sorry, Binti. You were saying?"

"It's okay. What about the metal?"

My father brought it to his teeth and bit the tip of one of the points. Then he touched it with the tip of his tongue and brought it so close to his left eye that he nearly touched his eyeball. He held it to his nose and sniffed. "I don't know this type of metal," he said. He smacked his lips. "It leaves a taste on the tongue, like when you taste the salts that gather on the Undying Trees during dry season."

The Undying Trees grew all over Osemba. They had thick rubbery wide leaves and trunks spiked with hard thorns that had lived longer than any generation could recall. Their ancient roots were so strong and they snaked so deeply beneath Osemba that the town's waterworks were not only built around them, they were built *along* them. The Undying Trees led the founders of Osemba to the only drinkable source of water for a hundred miles.

Nevertheless, the trees were strange. They vibrated so fast during thunderstorms that they made a howling sound, which permeated the city. During dry season, they produced salt on their leaves, which was used by healers to cure and treat all sorts of ailments. Life salt, it was called. The device I'd found tasted like life salt.

"It's an *edan*," my father said and I'd nodded like I'd never heard the word before. He explained to me that "*edan*" was a general name for devices too old for anyone to know their functions, so old that they were now more art than anything else. That's what my father wanted it for, as a piece of art to brag about to his friends. But I insisted on keeping it for myself and because he loved me, he let me.

Now here I was walking into the desert with the Desert People. How different my life would have been if my parents had just let me dance.

Lies

By sunup, I knew the Desert People had lied.

"Can you reach your Meduse?" my grandmother asked me. We'd walked through the remainder of the night and morning. Now, it was approaching midday and we stopped until night. We stood in the shade of one of the camels, some of the others bringing out dried dates and switching on noisy capture stations to collect water. I was nearly asleep on my feet, barely able to keep my eyes open. My grandmother's question woke me right up.

"Reach?" I asked. My eyes met Mwinyi's, who sat a few yards away crunching on what looked like dried leaves.

"Yes, speak to it," my grandmother said.

"I don't know," I muttered, looking out into the desert. "Maybe? Do I really—"

"Tell it that we will bring you back when we bring you back," my grandmother said. "Our village is three days' walk away."

"What? Why didn't you tell them this before? Why didn't you tell *me*?" I'd wondered why we were still walking when they'd promised to have me back by nightfall. It had been easier to stay in denial. I groaned. I'd gone from one extreme to another, days confined on a ship, then not even twenty-four hours later, days walking through open desert.

"Sometimes it's best to tell people what they need to hear," my grandmother said.

"Can't someone go back and tell them? I don't know if I can tell Okwu anything detailed," I breathed, my heart starting to beat the talking drum. "What if I can't do—"

"It's up to you, Binti," she said, dismissively. She spoke over her shoulder as she walked to two women who'd just set out a large bowl of dried dates. "You do it or you don't."

My grandmother wasn't offering me any real choice. If I didn't come home tonight, my family would fly into panic. Again. For the second time, they would be forced to deal with my disappearance and the fact that they couldn't do a thing about it. My mother would get terribly quiet and stop laughing, my father would work too hard in his shop, my siblings would feel an ache akin to one caused by the death of a loved one. Family. I had to reach Okwu.

However, I still didn't know much about my *okuoko*. I didn't understand how they affected me. How they connected me to the Meduse, especially Okwu. Why I could feel sensation through them. Why they writhed when I was furious. What I knew was that I could sense Okwu when I was on Math City and it was in Weapons City, which were hundreds of miles away and that I had once had a very weak but definite sense that the Meduse Chief who was planets away was checking up on me.

I could wiggle my *okuoko* on purpose, but I couldn't explain to anyone how I did it. It was like moving my nostrils, I just could. In this way, while petting the shaggy fur of the camel beside me, I reached out to Okwu. I thought about it, *willed* it. Seconds passed. Nothing. I sighed and glanced at my grandmother, who was watching me. I looked up into the blue sky and spotted a ship from afar that was leaving the atmosphere. A mere speck. The launch port was maybe a hundred miles away. I wondered if it was Third Fish. *No,* I thought. *Third Fish is giving birth soon.*

I shook my head. *Focus,* I thought. *Okwu.* I imagined the tent my father had set up outside the Root. How it was full of the gas the Meduse breathed. Okwu was the first of its kind on Earth since the Khoush-Meduse Wars. Okwu doing whatever Okwu did in its tent when it avoided interaction with any of my family or other curious Himba. And I softly slipped my mind into a set of equations that reminded me of space and movement across small lengths of it.

Now I reached out again, my hand flat on the camel's

rump, slowly moving up and down with its steady breathing. I strained to reach Okwu and it realized this and reached for me. I felt it grasp and suddenly I felt Okwu's mind. Sweat poured down my face and I felt all things around me tint Okwu's light blue.

Binti, I felt Okwu say through one of my *okuoko.* It vibrated against my left ear. *Where are you? You are far.*

In the hinterland, I responded. *I won't be back tonight.*

Do I need to come get you?

No.

Are you well?

Yes. The village is just far. Days away.

Okay. I will wait here.

Then just like that, Okwu let go and was gone. I came back to myself and my eyes focused on the desert before me.

"Done?" my grandmother asked. She stood behind me and I turned to her.

"Yes. It knows."

She nodded. "Well done," she said, holding her hands up and moving them around. She walked away.

~

They pitched their elaborate goatskin tents facing the desert to give everyone the semblance of privacy. Two men built a fire in the center of the tents and some of the women began to use it to cook. The soft whoosh of capture stations from behind two of the tents and their cool breath further cooled the entire camp. Soon, the large empty jug one of the camels had been carrying was rolled to the center of the tents and filled with water.

"You'll stay with me," my grandmother said, pointing to the tent two men had just set up for her. She handed me a cup. "Drink heavily, your body needs hydration." Inside, the tent was spacious and there were two bedrolls on opposite sides. For "dinner" there was flat bread with honey, a delicious strong-smelling hearty soup with dried fish, more dates, and mint tea. As the sun rose, everyone quickly disappeared into his or her tents to sleep.

I was pleasantly full and tired, but too restless to sleep just yet. So I sat on my mat, staring out at the desert, my grandmother snoring across from me. Since we'd walked into the desert, the flashbacks and day terrors I was used to having had disappeared. I inhaled the dry baking air and smiled. The healing properties of the desert had always been good for me. My eye fell on Mwinyi, who'd been watering the camels and now sat out on a sand dune facing the desert. His hands were working before him. I got up and walked over.

He looked at me as I approached, turned back to the desert, and continued working his hands. I paused, wondering if I was interrupting. I pushed on; I had to know. Plus, I'd seen several of them talking and laughing as they moved their hands like this, so I doubted it was like prayer or meditation.

"Hi," I said, hoping he'd stop moving his hands. He didn't.

"You should get some sleep," he said.

I cocked my head as I watched him. He was frowning as he pushed his blue sleeves back, held up his arms, and moved his hands in graceful swooping jabbing motions.

"I will," I said. I paused and took a breath. I wondered what would happen if I called up a current and connected it to his moving hands. Would the zap of it make him stop? "What is this that you're doing?" I blurted. "With your hands? Can you control it?" I waited, cringing as I bit my lip. For a moment, he only worked his hands, his eyes staring into the desert.

Then he looked up at me. "I'm communicating."

"But you do it when you . . . like now," I said as he did a flourish with his hands. "You're not talking to me right there. I don't understand it, if you are. And I see people doing it while talking to other people, too."

He looked at me for a long time and then glanced at the camp and then back at me.

"This is something your grandmother should tell you. Go ask her."

"I'm asking you," I said. "You all do it, so why can't I ask anyone?"

He sighed and muttered, "Okay, sit down."

I sat beside him, pulling my legs to my chest.

"Auntie Titi, your grandmother, is my grandfather's best friend," he said. "So I know all about your father and his shame. You have the same shame."

I blinked for a moment as two separate worlds tangled in my mind. Back when I was on the ship with the Meduse, they had referred to my *edan* as "shame" and now here was that word again, but in a completely different context. "I don't underst—"

"I saw how you looked at us," he said. "Just like every Himba I have ever encountered, like we're savages. You call us the 'Desert People,' mysterious uncivilized dark people of the sand."

I wanted to deny my prejudice, but he was right.

"Despite the fact that you're darker like us, have the crown like us, have our blood," he said. "I wonder how surprised you were when you saw that we could speak your language as well as our three languages. 'Desert People.' Do you even know the actual name of our tribe?"

I shook my head, slowly.

"We're the Enyi Zinariya," he said. "No, I won't translate that for you." He looked directly at me, into my eyes, and I didn't turn away. I wanted an answer to my initial question and I knew when I was being tested. There is nothing like being a harmonizer and looking directly into another harmonizer's eyes. Nothing.

Everything around us dropped away and there was a sonorous melody that vibrated between my ears that was so perfectly aligned that I felt as if I were beginning to float.

"I only know what I am taught," I whispered.

"That's not true," he said.

"I . . . I met one of you once," I said.

"We know," he said. "And was she a savage?"

"No," I said.

"So you knew that back then."

"Okay," I said, shutting my eyes and rubbing my forehead. "Okay."

He chuckled. "When we heard about what you did, we all cheered."

"Really?"

He turned away from me, finished talking. "You should go. Get some sleep."

"Answer my question first," I said. "Please."

"I did. I said we are communicating."

"With who?"

"Everyone."

"As you speak to me, you're speaking to others?"

"It's the same with your astrolabe," he said. "Can't you

use it while you talk to other people?"

"But no one is here."

"I was talking to my mother back in the village," he said. "She was asking about you."

"Oh," I said, frowning deeply. "So you can speak like how I speak to Okwu?"

He paused and moved his hands. Then he turned to me and flatly said, "Ask your grandmother."

I was about to get up, but then I stopped and asked, "Crown? You said I have the crown like you?"

He grasped a handful of his bushy red-brown hair, "This is the crown." Then he laughed. "Well, you used to have it. Before the Meduse took it and replaced it with tentacles."

I wanted to be offended but the way he said it, in such a literal way, instead pulled a hard laugh out of me and suddenly we were both giggling. When I calmed down, the fatigue of the journey hit me and I slowly got up. "What was the name of your clan again?" I asked.

"You're Himba, I'm Enyi Zinariya," he said.

"Enyi Zinariya," I repeated.

He nodded, smiling. "You pronounced it well."

"Okay," I said and went back to my grandmother's tent, lay down, and was asleep within seconds.

~

"Get up, girl."

I opened my eyes to my grandmother's face and the sound of the tent walls flapping from the wind. I stared into her eyes, blinking away the last remnants of sleep. When I sat up, I felt amazingly well rested. The cooling breeze of evening smelled so fresh that I flared my nostrils and inhaled deeply. I'd slept for nearly six hours.

My grandmother smiled, the strong breeze blowing her bushy hair about. "Yes, it's a good time to move across the desert."

The desert looked absolutely stunning, bright moonlight and the soft travel of the sand blending to make the ground look otherworldly. I could hear the others talking, laughing and moving about, and the two camels roaring as they were made to stand up. The smell of flat bread made my stomach grumble.

"Grandma," I said. "Please, tell me why the Enyi Zinariya speak with their hands."

Her eyes grew wide for a moment and I quickly said, "I've been planets away and learned about and met people from other worlds. It's wrong that I don't even know of my own . . . my own people." I let out a breath as my words sunk into me. They were the truth now, a truth that had been different a day ago when I had been ashamed and quiet about my blood. Seeing the Night Masquerade had lived up to its mythology. To see it *did* signify immediate drastic change.

"Walk with me," my grandmother said, then she left the tent. I followed, grabbing my satchel. As we walked away from the camp, I saw two of the men go to our tent and start breaking it down. She led me up the nearest high sand dune. When we reached the top, she turned toward the camp and sat down. I sat beside her. Below, the camp was aflutter with activity, all the tents packed up except ours. I was clearly the last to wake up.

"You've somehow learned the name of our clan."

"I asked Mwinyi."

"Having curiosity is the only way to learn," she said. She worked her hands before her for a moment and then looked at me. "That was me communicating with your father."

I raised my eyebrows.

"You Himba are so inward-looking," she said. "Cocooned around that pink lake, growing your technology from knowledge harvested from deep within your genius, you girls and women dig up your red clay and hide beneath it. You're an interesting people who have been on those lands for generations. But you're a young people. The Enyi Zinariya are old old Africans.

"And contrary to what you all believe, we have technology that puts yours to shame and we've had it for centuries." She paused, letting this news sink in. It wasn't sinking in to me easily. All that she'd said was so contrary to all that I had been taught that I'd begun to feel a little dizzy.

"We didn't create it, though," she continued. "It was brought to us by the Zinariya. Those who were there documented the Zinariya times, but the files were kept on paper and paper does not last. So all we really know is what elders read and then what the elders after those elders remembered and then what the next elders remembered and so on.

"The Zinariya came to us in the desert. They were a golden people, who glinted in the sun. They were solar and had landed in Earth's desert to rest and refuel on their way to Oomza Uni."

I couldn't control myself. "What?" I shrieked.

She chuckled. "Yes. We 'Desert People' knew of Oomza Uni before other people on Earth even had mobile phones!"

"Oh my goodness," I whispered. I couldn't imagine anyone on Earth back then being able to comprehend the very idea of Oomza Uni. Human beings on Earth hadn't even had real contact with people from outside yet, and the nonhumans who had had contact with extraterrestrials never bothered to convey anything to human beings. It was centuries later and I, who had been there, was still trying to wrap my brain around the sheer greatness of Oomza Uni.

"Our clan was even smaller and nomadic back then, and we became fast friends with the Zinariya. Though many of them left for Oomza within a few months, a few stayed with us for many years before going on to Oomza. Before leaving, they gave us something to help us communicate with them wherever they were and with each other wherever we were. They also called this 'zinariya.' It was a living organism tailored for our blood that every member of the clan drank into his or her system with water. Biological nanoids so tiny that they could comfortably embed themselves into our brains. Once you had them in you, it was like having an astrolabe in your nervous system. You could eat, hear, smell, see, feel, even *sense* it."

How had I not been able to guess this? Not that it was due to alien technology, but that they were working with a platform. They were manipulating a virtual platform like the ones astrolabes could project! One that only the Enyi Zinariya could see and access. I felt a sting of shame as I realized why I hadn't understood something so obvious. My own prejudice. I had been raised to view the Desert People, the Enyi Zinariya, as a primitive, savage people plagued by a genetic neurological disorder. So that's what I saw.

My grandmother nodded, a knowing smirk on her face. "And once the zinariya was in those who drank it, the nanoids were passed on to offspring through their DNA." She stopped talking and looked at me, waiting. Seconds passed and I frowned, anxious. I was about to ask if she'd told me all she was going to tell me when it exploded in my mind. My world went fuzzy for a moment and I was glad that I was sitting down. I shut my eyes and grasped at the first mathematical equation I could. Equations were always rotating around me like moons and this thought was soothing. Gently, I let myself tree. Then I opened my eyes, calm and balanced, and faced a very jarring bit of information.

"My father has the zinariya in him," I said.

My grandmother was looking at me, smirking. "Yes."

"And so do I and all my siblings."

"Yes."

"We carry alien technology."

"Yes."

The information tried to knock me down and I sunk deeper into meditation. If I wanted to, I could call up a current and send it streaming across the sand. *I am Himba,* I said to myself between the splitting and splitting fractals of equations, my most soothing pattern. *I am Himba, even if my hair has become* okuoko *because of my actions and even if I have Enyi Zinariya blood. Even if my DNA is alien.*

"Binti," my grandmother softly said.

"Why can't I see it? Why can't any of my siblings or my

father? None of us goes about waving our hands, manipulating objects that no one else can see."

"Your father can and does," she said. "When he so chooses. Didn't I tell you I'd just communicated with him? You think a son would abandon his mother? Just because he marries a Himba woman and decides to use his harmonizing skill in 'civilization' instead of the hinterland?"

I sighed and pressed my hands to my forehead. I felt so strange. This was all so strange.

"If you could reach my father, why'd you need me to reach out to Okwu?"

"To see if you could," she said, smiling.

I frowned.

"Now listen," she said. "The zinariya cannot just be used. It has to be switched on; it has to be activated. If it is not, you can live your whole life without even knowing it's in you. As you have."

"How does one switch it on?"

"The clan priestess does it. The Ariya. You will meet her tomorrow."

~

I wanted to turn back.

Oh, I wanted to turn back so badly. Enough was

enough was enough was enough. I could have made it home. Then I could have still made the trek out onto the salt trails on my own and caught up with the women and completed my pilgrimage. I could have become a whole woman in my clan, a complete Himba woman. All I had to do was walk into the darkness and use my astrolabe to tell me which way to go. However, we were days into the hinterland and if something did not kill me in the night, my lack of food or a proper water-gathering capture station would.

Plus, I didn't want to turn back. Why don't I ever want to do what I'm supposed to do?

~

So I went with Grandmother. I went with the Desert People.

It was another forty-eight hours of walking during the night, sleeping during the day, eating dates, flat bread, and palm-oil-rich Enyi Zinariya stews. Three more times, I saw Mwinyi protect us from packs of predatory animals—once from another pack of wild dogs and twice from hyenas. And I watched the Enyi Zinariya with new eyes; I especially watched their hands.

In the meantime, I barely touched my astrolabe. There

was so much around me to take in; I just didn't need it. Nor did I touch the pieces of my *edan*; I didn't want to think about it. Okwu checked on me once that second day and was even curter than it was the first time.

You okay, Binti?

Yes.

Good.

That was all. On the third, it didn't check in at all. I tried reaching it later that day as I had the first time, but it didn't respond. I wondered what it was doing back at the Root, but I wasn't worried. My grandmother was in touch with my father, so everyone knew everything anyway.

~

On the fourth night, the land changed. We simply came to the end of the sand dunes and the beginning of smooth white limestone. And soon after that, we reached a sudden drop and before I could understand what was happening and what I was seeing, I heard joyous ululating.

Gold People

The Enyi Zinariya lived in a vast network of caves in a huge limestone cliff. Within the bowels of these caves were winding staircases that led from cave to cave, family to family. Some caves were tiny, no larger than a closet, others were as vast as the Root. Upon arrival, I was taken for a quick tour of my grandmother's family's caves. I met so many of her people, young to old, all enthusiastically waving their hands about, that I could not understand the logic of where people lived.

It seemed everyone could stay wherever he or she was most comfortable, from child to elder. I saw a cave where an old man and his teenage granddaughter lived, the girl's parents (one of whom was the old man's daughter) living in a cave connected by a narrow tunnel. The old man and granddaughter were both obsessed with studying, collecting, and documenting stones, so their cave was full of stone piles and stacks of yellowing paper with scribbled research.

"Best to just have only one cave full of rocks," her mother told me with a laugh. "Those two are happy together." My grandmother's cave was tiny, but sparse and tidy with color-ful shaggy blue rugs, delicate mobiles hanging from the ceil-ing made of crystals one of her daughters had collected, and bottles of scented oils they specialized in making. The room also smelled immaculate.

It was brightly lit by a large circular solar lamp in the room's center. What was most striking was that my grandmother's cave was full of plants. It reminded me of one of the Third Fish's breathing rooms. There were pots with leafy green vines tumbling out of them hung near the high ceiling beside her bed. There were several large woven baskets full of sand with complex light green treelike succulents growing from them and dry biolu-minescent vines that grew directly on the cave's walls. Right there in the cave, my grandmother was growing five different types of tomatoes, three types of peppers, and some type of fruiting plant that I could not name.

"I'm a botanist," she said, putting her satchel down. "Your grandfather was, too."

"Was?"

She nodded. "He was Himba." And that was all she would say, though there was clearly so much more. I wanted to ask why he left the Himba and if he stayed in touch at all. I wanted to ask how he felt when my father decided to leave and return to the Himba. I wanted to ask if this was where my father had stayed when he was a child. I wanted to ask why she loved plants. I wanted to ask why she lived alone when everyone else in the village lived happily with many, even in the smaller caves. Instead, I looked at my grandmother's many thriving plants and breathed the lush air that smelled so different from the other caves and the dry desert outside.

I stopped at a small yellow flower growing from a dry root in a pot bigger than my hand. This was the same type of flower that had been growing on the *edan* years ago when I'd found it.

"What's this one?" I asked.

"I call it ola edo," she said. "Means 'hard to find, hard to grow.'" She laughed, "And not very pretty. Okay, time for you to rest, Binti. Tomorrow is your day."

As I had in the Third Fish's breathing chamber, I slept well here.

The Ariya

The Ariya's cave was a mile from the cave village in the center of a dried lake.

"Something used to live in it, back when this was a lake," Mwinyi said as we walked. "Maybe even dug the hole in the rock, itself."

"How do you know?" I said, looking at the ground as we walked. At some point, the smooth limestone had become craggy, making it hard to walk. I had to concentrate on not tripping over jutting rock.

"It's in the Collective," he said, glancing at me. "That's the Enyi Zinariya's memory that we all can touch."

I nodded.

"But no one knows exactly what kind of creature it was," he said. He waved his hands before him.

"Did you just tell her we're close?" I asked.

He looked sharply at me, frowning. "How'd you—"

"I'm not a fool," I said.

He grunted.

I laughed and pointed up ahead. "Plus, I see something just up there. A hole or something."

To call it a hole was to put it lightly. The opening in the hard ground was the size of a house. When we stepped up to it, I noticed two things. The first was that there was a large bird circling directly above the opening. The second was that rough stone steps were carved into the stone walls of the hole wound all the way to the bottom.

We descended the steps, Mwinyi going first. I ran my hand along the abrasive wall as I recited soft equations in my head. I called up a soft current and the mild friction from the current and my hand running over the coarse stone was pleasant beneath my fingertips. The deep cavern's walls were lined with books, so many books. The location of the sun must have been directly above, for the strong light of midday pleasantly flooded into the space. However, along with the light, bioluminescent vines grew in and lit the darker corners.

She stood in the shadows, beside a shelf of books, her arms crossed over her chest. "You haven't changed a bit," she said. Nearly a decade later, her bushy crown of hair a little grayer, her face a little wiser, and I still would know this woman anywhere. Could old women grow taller over the years?

"Hello, Mma," I said, looking up at her. I used the Himba term of respect because I didn't know what else to use.

"Binti," she said, pulling me into a tight hug. "Welcome to my home."

"Thank you for inviting me," I said.

She gave Mwinyi a tight hug, as well. "Thanks for bringing her. How was the walk?"

"As expected," he said.

"Come back for her at sundown."

"Ugh," I blurted, slumping. It was morning and I hadn't expected this to be an all-day thing. Though maybe I should have; springing things like this on me seemed to be the Enyi Zinariya way.

Mwinyi nodded, winked at me, and left.

She turned back to me. "Don't you know how to go with the flow yet?" she asked. "Adjust."

"I just didn't think that . . ."

"You saw the Night Masquerade," she said. "That's no small thing. Why expect what you expect?" Before I could answer, she said, "Come and sit down."

I took one more glance at Mwinyi, who was now near the top of the stairs, and followed the old woman.

We moved deeper into the cave and sat on a large round blue rug. It was cool and dark here, the air smelling sweet with incense. The place reminded me of a Seventh Temple, mostly empty and quiet. But *she* didn't remind me of a Seven priestess at all. She wasn't demure, she didn't cover her head with an orange scarf, she wore no *otjize*, and she got straight to the point. "Why do you think you saw the Night Masquerade?"

she asked. "You're not a man."

"Is it even real?" I asked.

"Don't answer a question with a question. Why do you think you saw it?"

"I don't know."

"Remember when we first met?"

"Yes."

"Why were you out there?"

"I found that place, I liked it," I said. "I wasn't supposed to be out there, I know."

"And look where it got you."

"What do you mean?"

"If you hadn't found the *edan*, would you have questioned and grown? Would you have gone? And even if you would have, would you be alive now?"

It came suddenly in that way that it had been for so many months. The rage. I felt it prick me like a needle in my back and my *okuoko* twitched. I took a deep breath, trying to calm it. "It doesn't matter," I muttered, my nostrils flaring.

"Why?"

Another wave of rage washed through my body and I angrily reached into my pocket, glad to have a reason to move. I felt my *okuoko* wildly writhing on my head and Ariya's eyes went to them, calmly watching their motion. *No matter*, I thought, bringing out the small pouch. I

leaned forward, breathing heavily through my flared nostrils, and wildly dumped it all out before her onto the carpet. The sound of tumbling metal pieces echoed and then
came a *thunk* as the golden grooved center fell out. I motioned to it with my hands to emphasize it all. "Because
I *broke* it!" I shouted, my voice cracking. "I broke it! I'm
a harmonizer and I de-harmonized an *edan*!" My voice
echoed around and up the cavern. Then silence.

I should have treed to calm myself. This was Ariya,
priestess of the Enyi Zinariya, I'd just met her, and here I
was behaving like a barbarian. "I know," I added. "I'm unclean. This was why I came home. For cleansing through
my pilgrimage. But I didn't go ... I'm here instead ..." I
trailed off and just watched her stare at the pieces and the
golden center. What felt like minutes passed, giving me
time to calm down. My *okuoko* grew still. The rest of my
body relaxed. And my *edan* was still broken. *I broke it*, I
thought.

"Unclean? No," Ariya finally said, shaking her head.
"That part of you that is Meduse now, you just need to get
that under control."

In one sentence, she explained something that had
been bothering me for a year. That's all it was. The random anger and wanting to be violent, that was just
Meduse genetics in me. *Nothing is wrong with me?* I
thought. *Not unclean? It's just ... a new part of me I need*

to learn to control? I'd come all this way to go on my pil-grimage because I'd thought my body was trying to tell me something was wrong with it. I hadn't wanted to ad-mit it to myself, but I'd thought I'd broken myself because of the choices I'd made, because of my actions, because I'd left my home to go to Oomza Uni. Because of guilt. The relief I felt was so all encompassing that I wanted to lie down on the rug and just sleep.

Ariya slowly got up, her knees creaking. She dusted off her long blue dress. "Sometimes, the obvious is too ob-vious," she muttered, walking away. Then over her shoul-der, she said, "Stay there."

I watched her ascend the stairs and when she reached the top, she walked off.

I lay on my back and sighed. "Just Meduse DNA," I muttered. "Or whatever it is they have for genetic code. That's all." I laughed, sitting up on my elbows. My eyes fell on the disassembled *edan* still lying on the rug. I stopped laughing.

~

She was gone for what might have been an hour. I'd dozed off right on that round blue rug, lulled by the cool darkness and incense. The sound of her sandals at the top of the stairs woke me. She stepped onto the first stair, paused, and then quickly descended. The moment her upper body came into sight, I saw the creature. Was I seeing what I was seeing? When she reached the bottom of the stairs, I stood up. It was an almost involuntary action. But what else was one to do when a great woman came down the stairs with a great owl perched on her arm?

The owl was about two feet tall with white and tan feathers, a black bill, a rounded frowning bushy eye-browed face, and wide yellow eyes. At the top of its head were brown and black feathers that looked like horns. Ariya's arm was protected by a brown leather armband, but that was all the protection she had. The owl could pluck out her eyes, slash her with its long white talons, slap her with its massive powerful wings if it wanted to. Instead, it stared at me with such intensity that I wondered if I should sit back down.

"If it's waiting outside, then it is right," she said. "It was right there when I came out. Help me."

I assisted as she slowly sat down with the owl perched on her arm. I sat across from them and gazed at the enormous bird.

"Is it heavy?" I asked

"Birds who spend most of their lives in the sky can't be heavy," she said. "No, this one is light as . . . a feather."

"Oh," I said.

"In my forty-five years as priestess, I have not done

this," she said. "Not even once."

Suddenly, I felt cold. Very very cold. With dismay. Deep down, I knew. From the moment my grandmother told me about the Zinariya, I'd known, really. Change was constant. Change was my destiny. Growth.

"Why?" I still asked.

"Because it's the only way you can fix it and you have to fix it, so you can use it to do what it needs to do." The owl hadn't taken its eyes off of me. "Do you know what zinariya means in the old language?"

I shook my head.

"It means 'gold.' That's the name we gave them because we couldn't speak their true name with our mouths and because that is what they were made of. Gold. Golden people. Their bodies, their ship, everything about them was gold. They came to the desert because they needed to rest and refuel and they loved the color of the sand . . . gold. Your *edan* is Zinariya technology; I knew this when I met you. I just thought, since it allowed you to find it, you could solve it without . . . without—"

"Needing to be activated."

She nodded. "No one who was not one of us has ever known about the zinariya and those who marry out or leave, they're so ashamed of being Enyi Zinariya that they don't tell their families."

"Like my father," I said. "It's like having some genetic

disease, in a way. If Himba or Khoush knew of it, they'd ..."

Ariya smiled. "Oh, they know, someone in those clans knows enough to build toxic ideas against us right into their cultures. That's really why we are so outcast, untouchable to them. To Himba and Khoush we are the savage 'Desert People,' not the Enyi Zinariya. No one wants our blood in their line. Anyway, the Collective knows the names and faces of all your siblings and their children."

"Oh," I said, feeling a little better. "Well, that is good."

"But that's all."

We stared at each other for a moment.

"Do you want to do this?" she asked.

"Do I need to?"

"Hmm. You're still ashamed of what you are."

"No," I said. "I'm Himba and proud of that."

She raised her eyebrows. "Not your grandmother. She is Enyi Zinariya. And we are a matriarchal clan, so your father is, too."

"No," I snapped. "Papa is Himba." I could feel the sting of my own nearsightedness. It was irritating and pushing me off-balance in a way that made it hard for me to think. My confusion evoked a flash of Meduse anger.

"Do you want it?" she asked.

I opened my mouth to answer, but I didn't speak it because what I'd have spoken was stupid. It was wrong. But it was the truth, too. If I went through with this, I was taking another step outside what it was to be Himba, away from myself, away from my family. I wanted to hide from the owl's unwavering gaze.

"Do you want it?" she asked again.

I sighed loudly and shook my head. "Priestess Ariya, I don't understand any of this. If the *edan* is Zinariya technology, why does the outer metal kill Meduse? I'm part Meduse now, so why doesn't my edan kill me? I don't understand what is happening to me, why my *edan* fell apart, what that ball is, why it matters, why I'm here! I came here to go on pilgrimage; I'm not even there. I'm here. I don't know what I'm doing or where I'm going!" I stared at her with wide eyes, breathing heavily. I couldn't breathe. I couldn't think. I couldn't tree.

I was seeing all the Khoush in the dining room on the Third Fish. Dead. Chests burst open by the stingers of Meduse. *Moojh-ha ki-bira,* the "great wave." The flow of death like water I'd fallen into that in some twisted way gave me a new life. I leaned to the side, pressing my hand to my chest. Angry tears stung my eyes. How could Okwu have been a part of this slaughter? Why did the Seven allow this to happen? Yet, drowning in the waters of death gave me new life. Not drowning in it, carried by it.

"Shallow breaths, increased heart rate, you're having a panic attack," my astrolabe in my pocket announced in its stiff female voice. "I suggest you drop into mathematical meditation." I wanted to smash it to bits.

The priestess did nothing but watch me. The owl puffed out its throat and hooted three times. Soft and peaceful. My eyes wide as I stared into the owl's, I inhaled a deep breath, filling my lungs to full capacity. When I exhaled, the owl hooted softly again and the sound calmed me more. Then it hooted again, leaning down and bringing its neck low near its feathery legs, as it held my eyes. Soon the panic attack passed.

"Do you want it?" Ariya asked a fourth time.

The voice came from deep in me, but it was familiar. I'd been hearing it since I left home, ignoring its steady matter-of-fact low voice: "You did not succeed your father. No man will marry you. Selfish girl. Failed girl." I was supposed to be these things in order to be. I had not taken my place within the collective. This had left me feeling exposed and foundationless, even as I pursued my dreams. Now here I was about to make another choice that would further ensure I could never go back.

I shut my eyes and thought of Dele, who'd been my friend but had looked at me like a pariah when we'd last spoken. His judgment and rejection had stung me in a way I'd not been prepared for and reminded me that I'd made my choice. And my choice had been to come home. *Dele has always seen things so simply,* I thought. *Even when they're infinitely complex. He's not a harmonizer.* I opened my eyes and looked at Ariya.

"What will it . . . do?" I breathed.

"Connect you to an entire people and a memory. And allow you to solve your *edan*."

"I'll be a desert person," I moaned. I blinked, wanting to kick myself. "I'm sorry. I meant to say Enyi Zinariya. Himba people see you as savages. I've already been changed by the Meduse. Now I'll never . . ."

"What will you be?" she asked. "Maybe it is not up to you."

I looked at my hands, wanting to bring them to my face and inhale the scent of the *otjize* covering them. I wanted to go home. I wanted to chase crabs near the lake until the sun set and then turn around to look at the Root and admire the glow of the bioluminescent plants that grew near the roof. I wanted to argue with my sisters in the living room. I wanted to walk into the village square with my best friend Dele to buy olives. I wanted to sit in my father's shop and construct an astrolabe so sophisticated, my father would clap arthritis-free hands with delight. I wanted to play math games with my mother where sometimes she'd win and sometimes I'd win. I wanted to go home.

More tears rolled down my face as I realized I'd left my jar of *otjize* in my grandmother's cave with my other things. I flared my nostrils and squinted in an attempt to prevent any more tears from falling. It worked. I steadied. I was clear now. I wanted to go home, but I wanted to solve the *edan* more. Everything comes with a sacrifice. I wiped my face with my hand and looked at my *otjize*-stained palm. "Okay," I whispered. I straightened my back. "What's the owl for?" I asked in a strained voice.

"I'm no mathematical harmonizer, but Mwinyi told me what treeing feels like, what it does." She paused. "I suggest you do that when I start. From the start. Do it while you are calm."

"Okay," I said. "But what of the owl?"

"She's not an owl," Ariya said.

Initiative

"Drink this," she said, handing me the clay cup.

It tasted both sweet and smoky, and as I swallowed the liquid it coated my throat and warmed my belly. She took the cup from me and set it on the ground beside her. We were sitting outside in the hot sun, not far from the lip of the underground cave. Here, I really noticed the soft whoosh of the air moving up and out of the cave. Above, the owl flew in wide circles.

Ariya handed me the long feather the owl had allowed her to pluck from its wing. When she'd taken it from the owl, it had flapped its wing right after she'd plucked it, as if it were in pain and trying to beat the pain away. When she handed it to me, I noticed that the end of the feather was needle sharp.

"She has no name," Ariya now said. "But she's the only animal alive from back when the Zinariya were among us. She used to live with the one that gave the zinariya to the first group of us. They had no clear leader and were all so connected that you couldn't tell them apart, except for that particular one who was always with this creature.

Today, she looks like a horned owl, but there are other days . . . when she does not. Anyway, when they left, she was given many things, including a task."

I looked at the feather tip. In the sunlight, it glinted the tiniest bit; it was wet with something.

"Prick your fingertip with it," she said. "Hard. Then hold it there."

I bit my lip. I didn't like doing harm to myself on purpose or accidentally.

"It has to be you who does it. Your choice. There are catalysts in the feather and they need to enter your bloodstream."

"Okay," I whispered. But before I did, I said, "$Z = z^2 + c$." It split and split and split in its lovely complex and convoluted way. Faster and faster, until I saw the coiling design in my mind and before me. Soon that became a current. A soft blue current that I harmonized with a second current I called up from the same equation. With my mind, I asked them to wrap around me, to protect me. And in the sunshine in the middle of the hinterland, as the priestess of the Desert People who were the Enyi Zinariya watched, I plunged the sharp tip of the feather into the flesh of my left thumb.

In the stories of the Seven, life originated from the rich red clay that had soaked up rains. Microorganisms were called into active being when one of the Seven willed it and the others became interested in what would happen. That clay was Mother, *otjize*. I was clay now. I was watching from afar, feeling nothing, but able to control. I held the feather to my finger. And then, from that place waving with equations, the blue currents braiding around each other connecting around me, my body acted without my command.

When I was five, I had asked my mother what it was like to give birth. She smiled and said that giving birth was the act of stepping back and letting your body take over. That childbirth was only one of thousands of things the body could do without the spirit. I remember asking, "If you step away from your body to give birth, then who is there doing the birthing?" I wondered this now, as my body acted.

I couldn't see it happening, but I could distantly sense it—my body was pulling something, energy from the ground. From the earth, from deep. My body was touching the Mother, nudging her awake, and then telling her to come. *The Seven are great,* I thought. This was not my pilgrimage where I would have honored the Seven and entered the space only those who have earned the right could enter. I would probably never have that now. This was something else.

The Mother came.

I was treeing, but now I felt her fully. My entire body

was alight. If I had not been treeing, what would have been left of my sanity? How could those who could not tree ever go through this? The glow within me became a shine that engulfed me, one that took on the color of the currents I still circulated. For a moment, I glimpsed up at Ariya and met her wide surprised eyes. I was reminded of my teacher Professor Okpala back on Oomza Uni that day I saw . . .

Iridescent white lights drowned it all out, through a jellylike substance.

Then darkness.

Then I was there again . . .

. . . I was in space. Infinite blackness. Weightless. Flying, falling, ascending, traveling, through a planet's ring of brittle metallic dust. It pelted my flesh like chips of glittery ice. I opened my mouth a bit to breathe, the dust hitting my lips. Could I breathe? Living breath bloomed in my chest from within me and I felt my lungs expand, filling with it. I relaxed.

"Who are you?" a voice asked. It spoke in the dialect of my family and it came from everywhere . . .

I fell out of the tree.

My *okuoko* were writhing. Then . . . rain? Wetness? Something was tearing. I was coughing, as I inhaled what my lungs could not tolerate. The gas was all around me, then it was not. I inhaled deeply, again, filling my lungs with air this time.

I opened my eyes wide. To the desert. And the smell of smoke. Ariya was feet away, her mouth open with shock, as she smacked at her garments. Smoke was rising all around her. She was putting out fire. Her clothes were burning. *From my current?* I wildly wondered. *Did I lose control of it?* Never in my life had I done such a thing.

I put a hand out to hold myself up. As a harmonizer, you saw numbers and equations in everything, circulating around you like the eye floaters you see on the surface of your eye if you pay too close attention. I was used to that. However, what I was seeing now was alien. Circles of various proportions from the size of a pea to that of a large tomato, and various colors all arranged in an order, all around me. They pulsed, becoming transparent and then solid, with each breath, with each movement, with each of my thoughts. Nevertheless, there was something far more urgent that I had to deal with.

"Okwu," I said, staring at Ariya. My heart felt as if it were slashing up the inside of my chest. "My Meduse. Have they killed it? I have to go back."

Ariya said nothing. I got up on shaky legs. "I have to go," I said, tears filling my eyes. I turned and looked in the direction Mwinyi had brought me. From afar, I could see a glimpse of the village caves. I took a step when I noticed something falling out of the sky. It was red orange, like my *otjize,* and it was on fire. It came right at me and I would never be able to outrun it.

I turned to it. *Let it slam into me and burn me to cinders,* I thought. *Let it.* I watched the fireball hurl toward me. I submitted to my death, as I had submitted to it on the ship when the Meduse had killed everyone. I felt its heat bear down on me and a blast of wind blew past me that was so strong I stumbled and sat down hard on the ground. The pain of it shook me from my hysteria. I blinked away the sandy tears in my eyes. They'd mixed with my *otjize,* sweat and sand on my skin.

Ariya slowly came to me. "Calm yourself," she harshly said. She was carrying her walking stick. *When had she gotten that?* And now, she was leaning on it. "Binti, you have to calm yourself." The old woman looked toward the village then at me. "You have just been initiated," she said. "*I* threw that fireball at you to snap you out of it."

"You?"

"Hold your hands up," she said. She held both her hands before her. "Like this. See them. Your will controls the controls. You make them come and go."

I held my hands up and there were the colored circles again. This time right before my face and solid like hard honey candies. I slowly reached out to it, expecting my hand to pass right through. I tapped on it and I heard the light *tick tick* of my nail against thin hard material. I pressed it and the words *Like this. See them. Your will con-*

trols the controls. You make them come and go scrolled out about a foot from my face in *otjize* red-orange loopy Otji-himba writing.

I touched the words and they faded away like incense smoke and I could softly hear Ariya speak those same words again.

"What is—"

"It's zinariya," Ariya said. "You're now one of us."

I pressed my hands to the sides of my head, as if I could stop that which I couldn't stop. Just like the strange sensation of my *okuoko* when I first felt them, this was ... this was beautiful. I felt the pain and glory of growth, was straining and shuddering with it. The stress of it caused a ringing in my ears as I looked around, thinking hard. Then I was seeing the words. *Binti? Why are you ... is that you? Why are you ... have they ... Oh no, no, no, what have you done?*

I sat there, a sob caught in my throat. Even in that moment of strangeness, the utter dismay so clear in his words made my heart sink. I felt a powerful regret and wished I had not had the zinariya activated. Anything to not inspire such disappointment in my father, after all I'd already done to him, to everyone, to myself. I fought for focus. "Papa!" I shouted. "What is happening? What happened?"

"He won't hear you," Ariya said. "You have to *send*."

Astrolabe, I thought frantically. *Like astrolabe. But more primitive.* I couldn't see him but I could "send" to him. I did it intuitively, imagining I was using the holographic mode of my astrolabe where it would project a page in the air, type onto it, and move things around. As I did so, I was vaguely aware of the fact that I was doing those hand movements the Enyi Zinariya were known for, like a madwoman. And at the moment, I was.

Papa, I sent. *What has happened? What happened to Okwu? Where are you? I am in the hinterland.*

His answer came immediately. *Why did you allow this? You used to be such a beautiful girl.* His words hit me like a slap and I felt it slip through my body and for a moment, I forgot everything. I rubbed my forehead then ran a finger over my *okuoko. Mine,* I thought. *These are mine.* I raised my hands and wrote, *Papa, I'm fine. Please, what is happening?*

There was a long pause before the words came. And when they came, I sat back down on the ground and the words moved down with me. *We can't get out. The Khoush have set fire to the Root. We cannot get out. But the walls will protect us. The Root is the root. We will be okay. Stay where you are.*

Papa! I sent. I sent again and again, but he did not respond. My words wouldn't even melt away. They wouldn't go! I shuddered with rage and then grabbed some sand and threw it, screaming, tears flying from my eyes. I stared out into the desert for a long moment. I stared and stared. Sand and sky, sky and sand. I tried to reach Okwu. Again, nothing.

I dropped into meditation, the numbers flew like water, the controls faded but did not disappear, the *okuoko* on my head writhed. I stood up. "I'm going home," I told Ariya. She only nodded, her attention on the figure coming up the desert. It was Mwinyi and he was leading a camel. "You'll go with him," Ariya said.

"The Enyi Zinariya won't come with us?" I asked.

She only looked at me. Then she said, "We'd come if there was a fight to fight."

I didn't ask her what she meant. Above, the owl circled.

~

When Mwinyi and I climbed onto the camel and got moving, the owl followed us overhead for several miles. Then it turned back. It returned to Ariya, I assumed. Its job was complete. I was Himba, a master harmonizer. Then I was also Meduse, anger vibrating in my *okuoko*. Now I was also Enyi Zinariya, of the Desert People gifted with alien technology. I was worlds. What was home? Where was home? Was home on fire? I considered these things as Mwinyi and I rode. But not for very long. Mwinyi had brought my satchel and now I reached into it. I worked my fingers into the pouch to touch the metal pieces of my still broken *edan*. I grasped the grooved golden ball. It was warm.

There was no fight to fight, Ariya had said. *We'll see,* I thought, grasping the huge camel's thick coarse fur. *We will see.*